**Tony could see his reflection.
But where the vampire should have been,
the mirror was empty!**

He spun around—and there was the vampire, large as life, with his tousled hair hanging to his shoulders, and his grubby cape with its moth holes. Tony gulped. He knew very well that a vampire's image doesn't reflect in a mirror. But there was a big difference between reading about it in a book and actually finding it was true in real life. But then he giggled. After all, this wasn't just any old vampire, it was Rudolph Sackville-Bagg, his best friend. There was no reason to be scared of him—was there?

Books by Angela Sommer-Bodenburg

MY FRIEND THE VAMPIRE
THE VAMPIRE MOVES IN
THE VAMPIRE TAKES A TRIP
THE VAMPIRE ON THE FARM

Available from MINSTREL Books

THE VAMPIRE ON THE FARM

ANGELA SOMMER-BODENBURG

pictures by Amelie Glienke

A MINSTREL® BOOK

PUBLISHED BY POCKET BOOKS

New York   London   Toronto   Sydney   Tokyo   Singapore

This book is for Burghardt Bodenburg, who is heartily annoyed because Boris has overtaken him in the race to grow vampire teeth—and for Katja, who still has no gaps in her baby teeth.

—Angela Sommer-Bodenburg

This book is a work of fiction. Names, characters, places and incidents are either the product of the author's imagination or are used fictitiously. Any resemblance to actual events or locales or persons, living or dead, is entirely coincidental.

A Minstrel Book published by
POCKET BOOKS, a division of Simon & Schuster Inc.
1230 Avenue of the Americas, New York, NY 10020

This translation copyright © 1985 by Andersen Press Ltd.
First published in German in 1983 as *Der kleine Vampir auf dem Bauernhof*
© 1983 by Rowohlt Taschenbuch Verlag, Reinbek bei Hamburg, West Germany

ISBN: 0-671-70236-X

First Minstrel Books printing October 1990

10 9 8 7 6 5 4 3 2 1

A MINSTREL BOOK and colophon are registered trademarks
of Simon & Schuster Inc.

Printed in the U.S.A.

Contents

THE VAMPIRE ON THE FARM

1 / Country Air

"Isn't it gorgeous here!" exclaimed Tony's mother. Tony smothered a giggle as he watched her put her suitcase down on the dusty ground right next to some dried-up cow dung.

"Real pretty," he muttered, looking over toward the farmhouse. To think he was stuck here for a whole week with his parents, who had picked out this stupid farm all by themselves!

A farm vacation—yuck! Of course, they hadn't bothered to ask him if he wanted to spend his vacation staring at a bunch of pigs and chickens. And for *real* excitement he was supposed to go for nice walks and breathe in the fresh country air. Double yuck!

"Anyway," he said to his parents, "you must be pretty disappointed about the fresh country air." Tony had spotted some more dung that wasn't nearly as dried up. "It stinks around here!"

"It doesn't at all!" contradicted his mother. "I think the air is wonderful. So healthy! And so much cleaner than the air back home in the city. Don't you think so, dear?" She turned to Tony's father, who was unloading luggage from the trunk of the car.

"It smells terrific," he replied, breathing deeply.

"Well, I think it stinks," Tony persisted. "The air may be healthy, but it sure stinks."

His mother glared at him. "Oh, excuse me! And

when did you develop such a sensitive nose? When I think of that friend of yours, that Rudolph Sackville-Bagg . . ."

"What about him?"

"Talk about stink!" exclaimed his mother. "That silly cape he gave you smelled like it hadn't been washed in months."

Tony couldn't help grinning. "That cape was a hundred years old, Mom, maybe even older." Teasingly he added, "And of course, vampires never wash their capes."

Tony knew perfectly well that his parents didn't believe in vampires. So naturally whenever he said anything about his friend the little vampire, they thought he was making up stories. That's why he usually told the truth if his parents asked him about Rudolph—since the truth was the last thing they'd believe. It was no different this time.

"You and your vampires," groaned his mother. "We're in the country now. And I intend to have a nice vacation from your endless vampires—vampires on TV, vampires in the movies, vampires in all of those awful books you read!"

"Okay, no more vampires," said Tony, trying not to laugh. How could she know that last night Tony and Rudolph had sneaked aboard a train and smuggled a coffin all the way from the city to Lower Bogsbottom? What *would* Tony's mother say if she knew that somewhere on this very farm, the little vampire was sleeping peacefully away in his coffin?

"I'll help with the luggage," he said cheerfully. He

picked up a suitcase and two bags and carried them to the door of the farmhouse.

"Now, why is he so enthusiastic all of a sudden?" he heard his father say.

"He can't stand it when I make fun of his vampire stories," his mother replied. "He's probably dreaming up a horrible new one right now to pay me back!"

2 / Rustic Decorations

Tony had been crazy about vampire stories even before he met Rudolph Sackville-Bagg and his little sister, Anna, who lived with their vampire family in the Sackville-Bagg vault. If you could call that living! thought Tony. All day long they slept like corpses in their coffins. It was only when the sun went down that they woke up and left their coffins under cover of darkness to go off hunting—hunting for human blood!

Tony shuddered. Even here, in the sunny guest room, it gave him goose bumps to think of the vampires' favorite food. And it made his hair stand on end to think of the little vampire's bloodthirsty relatives: Frederick the Frightful, Thelma the Thirsty, Sabina the Sinister, Gruesome Gregory, George the Boisterous—and the worst of them all, Aunt Dorothy the Dreadful!

Just then there was a knock on his door. Tony gave a startled jump. "Y-yes?" he asked hesitantly. The door opened and his father came in.

"Oh, it's you," said Tony, relieved. For a second he had really thought Aunt Dorothy might be standing outside his door, even though that couldn't be possible. After all, it wasn't even noon yet.

"Mrs. Minnowpail wants to give us a tour of the farm," announced Tony's father.

"I still have to unpack."

"How do you like your room?" asked his father, looking around. Without waiting for Tony's reply, he declared, "Hey, this is pretty cozy!"

"For a girl," muttered Tony under his breath. The wardrobe with its hand-painted rustic decorations, the old-fashioned bed, and the flowery curtains at the window weren't exactly to his taste.

"Did you know that Mrs. Minnowpail did all the decorating herself?"

"No kidding," said Tony indifferently.

"I wish I'd had all this when I was your age! A real vacation on a farm, and even a room of my own! Do you know what I used to call a vacation?"

"No."

"A day swimming at the old gravel pits not far from where we lived. We had to ride our bikes all the way there and back, and all we had to spend was a nickel apiece for ice cream."

Tony groaned softly. When his dad started telling one of his old-days stories, it was best not to say anything to encourage him. Otherwise the story would last all day!

"But we had lots of fun roughing it in the old days. Nowadays, on the other hand, everybody wants to go to some fancy resort, preferably with two swimming pools and a video-game lounge."

Exactly, agreed Tony silently as he put his clean socks and his bathing suit into the wardrobe.

"But we can still have fun roughing it. Isn't that right, Tony?" His father had the goofy, faraway look on his face that he always got when he told one of his old-days stories.

"Uh, sure, Dad," muttered Tony, sliding his empty duffel bag under the bed. Then he quickly carried his backpack to the wardrobe. He couldn't very well unpack it in front of his father, since that was where he'd hidden the little vampire's spare cape under some schoolbooks. He slipped the backpack into the wardrobe and closed the door.

"Okay, Dad. Now I'm ready for some fun," said Tony with a grin.

3 / Tony the Sensitive

Mrs. Minnowpail was standing in the yard talking to Tony's mother. She had short blond hair and she was wearing jazzy riding boots and brand-new jeans. Tony didn't think she looked at all like a farm woman.

"How do you like your room?" she asked him with a smile.

Why did grown-ups always have to ask the same question!

"It's real cozy," said Tony, trying to be polite.

"In fact, it's Joanna's room," she said, "but when we have guests, she sleeps in the top bunk in Jeremy's room. I hope it's not too frilly for you."

"Oh, Tony isn't sensitive about things like that," declared his mother. "As a matter of fact he has a great deal of respect for girls. I'm sure he's looking forward to getting to know Joanna while we're here."

"What?" croaked Tony, blushing furiously. He couldn't believe his mother had said that! He was totally sensitive about *anything* to do with girls—especially meeting them!

"Joanna's away this weekend. She and Jeremy are visiting their grandparents," explained Mrs. Minnowpail.

"What a shame," said Tony's father. "Tony won't have anyone to play with."

"I can take care of myself," said Tony irritably.

9

He'd seen Jeremy and Joanna briefly the day his parents dragged him along to the farm to reserve the rooms for this dumb vacation. He certainly wouldn't miss Jeremy, whose hobby was collecting toy knights in armor. Yuck! And the last thing he wanted to do was get to know Joanna!

"Are Jeremy and Joanna on vacation now too?" asked Tony's mother.

"No, not for another week yet."

Tony gave a quiet sigh of relief. That meant he'd be on his own at least until the little Minnowpails came home from school.

"Now I'll show you around the farm!" Mrs. Minnowpail opened a wooden door painted green. "This way to the cowshed," she called gaily.

Tony's parents hurried after her—as happy and excited as if they'd never seen a cow before, thought Tony scornfully. He followed behind them at a more dignified pace. Drooling over cows was kid stuff, and he was much too old for that!

4 / Cattle

Tony practically burst out laughing inside the cow shed. The cow dung smelled a million times worse than Rudolph's cape, and there wasn't even a single cow in the shed! The only animal in sight was a gray cat, who was sitting on a wooden beam washing itself. Tony looked over at his parents with a mocking grin.

"Love the cows," he said smugly.

"Did you think they'd be inside all day?" asked Mrs. Minnowpail.

"Why not? They have to be milked, don't they?"

"Milked? I should say not." Mrs. Minnowpail began to laugh. "We keep *bulls,* not cows. And right now they're out in the field."

Tony could feel his face getting red. How was he supposed to know that? Anyway, he wasn't the least bit interested in cattle.

"Don't you have any other animals?" he blurted out.

"Of course, we do." Mrs. Minnowpail went over to a little wooden partition. "Come and meet our baby lamb. He was very weak at birth, so we've had to bottle-feed him. His name is Ali Bahbah."

Tony almost said, "How cute!" but just managed to stop himself. After all, only little kids went ga-ga over cute little baby animals!

Tony's parents stroked the little lamb.

"Wouldn't you like to pet him?" asked Mrs. Minnowpail.

"No," he muttered, and stuck his hands firmly into the pockets of his overalls.

"Tony thinks he's too old for that sort of thing," said his father.

"Is that so?" snarled Tony. "I thought you'd never notice!"

"Tony Noodleman!" exclaimed his mother heatedly. "What's gotten into you?"

Suddenly all the anger Tony felt about being stuck on the farm rose up in him.

"Look—stroking baby animals or oohing and aahing over horses—little boys and girls may think all that's fantastic. But I don't!"

He abruptly turned away because he felt tears welling up in his eyes. He couldn't care less anymore if his parents were mad at him.

There was a painful silence. Then he heard his father ask, "Maybe there are some bats somewhere? Tony's crazy about bats and vampires, you know."

"Bats?" said Mrs. Minnowpail. "There are a couple over in the barn. Would you like to go see them?"

"Oh, no, I wouldn't!" said Tony's mother. "Just once I'd like to spend a whole week having nothing to do with vampires or bats."

Tony breathed a sigh of relief. He didn't want his mother or anyone else poking around the barn—not when he was almost certain that Rudolph had hidden his coffin there last night.

"Jeremy is mad about knights in armor," said Mrs. Minnowpail. "Every child is crazy about something."

"It isn't the same sort of thing at all!" Tony blurted out, and immediately wished he hadn't.

"Why, what's the big difference?" Mrs. Minnowpail asked.

"Because—" Tony hesitated. He certainly didn't want to give Rudolph away.

"Tony believes in vampires," his father explained. "He even has a friend who he says *is* a vampire."

Mrs. Minnowpail laughed. "Then I guess I should be grateful that Jeremy only plays with toy knights and doesn't try to go jousting himself."

Tony was seething furiously, but this time he kept it inside. Let them laugh—all it meant was that they didn't suspect a thing!

5 / The Chicken-coop Kid

"It says in your brochure that you have pigs too," said Tony's mother.

"That's right, pigs for fattening," confirmed Mrs. Minnowpail. "But they'll be more interesting at feeding time. My husband takes care of that at six o'clock, and you can see them then."

Tony stood and yawned. Pigs—big deal! They probably smelled even worse than the cow shed.

"How about a look at the chickens instead?" suggested Mrs. Minnowpail. With a glance at Tony she added, "I think you might like our peacock."

"Maybe," said Tony in a bored voice.

But he was impressed in spite of himself when he saw the peacock lifting its tail feathers to form a huge, magnificently colored wheel. Suddenly it gave a piercing cry that sent shudders right through Tony. It was the most frightening sound he'd ever heard. Luckily the peacock was behind the high wire fence that surrounded the chicken coop.

"Uncanny sound, isn't it?" remarked Mrs. Minnowpail. "Sometimes it even wakes us up."

"It does that at night too?" gasped Tony. He immediately thought of the little vampire, who knew only about bats and owls. If the peacock's terrifying cry rang out at night while Rudolph was flying around, he'd probably get so scared that he'd crash and break a leg! Tony had to be sure to warn Rudolph as soon as they met that evening.

Besides the peacock there were chickens—at least thirty of them. Mrs. Minnowpail threw them a handful of corn, and they came rushing over, cackling and squawking.

His parents smiled. Tony stepped back from the fence nervously. He didn't see what was so funny about a bunch of chickens!

"Don't you like chickens either?" asked Mrs. Minnowpail.

"I *love* them," answered Tony, "with mashed potatoes and gravy."

"Tony, behave yourself!" exclaimed his mother, but Mrs. Minnowpail just smiled. She pointed to a little hut in the middle of the fenced-in area. "If you're so fond of chickens, you ought to take a look at the laying hens. They sit on their eggs in that coop until the chicks hatch."

With these words she opened a gate in the fence and gently pushed Tony inside. Suddenly he found himself surrounded by the startled chickens. He hopped from one foot to the other, terrified that they might peck him in the leg.

"Relax," Mrs. Minnowpail said with a laugh. "They won't do anything to you!"

"That's easy for you to say!" retorted Tony. Once he'd seen a scary movie about birds attacking human beings, and at that very moment the picture of those hacking beaks was flashing through his mind.

"He's not afraid of vampires—but chickens are

another story!" mocked his father from the other side of the fence.

Tony glared at him. "I'm just being careful!" he said through clenched teeth.

Slowly he made his way back to the gate. He kept his eye on the chickens the whole time, just to make sure they didn't get worked up into a frenzy like the birds in the film. But the chickens just scratched around in the dirt and pecked at the corn. Luckily he had just about reached the gate when the peacock gave a cry so loud and shrill that Tony almost wet his pants! In a flash he was through the gate, and with a huge sigh of relief he slammed it shut behind him.

"Let's hear it for the Chicken-coop Kid!" teased his father.

Tony scowled. With long strides he stalked over to a jungle gym that stood on a patch of grass near the fence, pulled himself up, and perched on the top.

"All right, go ahead and laugh!" he called.

"You'll get used to farm life in no time," said Mrs. Minnowpail. "Even to chickens," she added with a smile. "Come on, now I'll show you the horses."

"Horses!" repeated Tony with a groan.

"Yes," said Mrs. Minnowpail enthusiastically. "Blackie, the one we ride, and her foal, Tinka."

Tony hesitated. But after his performance with the chickens he wasn't about to admit that he was afraid of horses too. "Well, okay," he said, "but the horses are absolutely the last animals I'm going to look at."

"Until after lunch," replied Mrs. Minnowpail, laughing. "Ready, cowboy?"

6 / Giddyap!

Tony jumped down from the jungle gym and followed Mrs. Minnowpail and his parents. They all stopped in front of a low wooden fence.

"Blackie!" called Mrs. Minnowpail.

To Tony's surprise a white horse came trotting up to the fence, followed by a little brown foal. While Mrs. Minnowpail was talking to the horses, Tony watched and thought how silly it was to chatter at horses as if they were people. When Blackie began to whinny softly, Mrs. Minnowpail took an apple from her pocket and held it out to Tony.

"Here, give this to Blackie."

"Me?"

"Yes. Then she'll get to know you, and she won't be nervous the first time you ride her."

"But I don't want to ride her," said Tony as calmly as he could.

"You don't want to ride? But all our guests want to ride! You like horses, don't you?"

"Uh, yes," said Tony uncertainly.

"Of course you do. Now, give Blackie her apple. She's getting impatient."

Cautiously Tony stretched out his hand. The huge head came nearer. Its mouth opened. Tony saw two rows of enormous teeth. . . . He couldn't help it: His hand shook, and the apple fell onto the grass.

Mrs. Minnowpail picked it up and gave it to Blackie. "Blackie doesn't bite. Do you, Blackie?" she said, turning to the horse. "You're the kindest, friendliest horse on the farm, aren't you?"

"Tony's a little nervous. It's the first time he's ever been on a farm," explained Tony's mother.

"And the last!" said Tony decisively.

"Tony, please!" exclaimed his mother.

Mrs. Minnowpail seemed unruffled. "The first day is always the hardest for first-timers. By tomorrow you'll be acting like an old farmhand. Now, let me see." She studied Tony's clothes and nodded approvingly. "Overalls and boots—that's exactly what I like to wear when I ride. How about giving it a try?"

Tony looked imploringly at his mother. Maybe she'd tell him not to ride. After all, he was wearing his brand-new boots, and they might get scuffed. But all she said was "Didn't you hear Mrs. Minnowpail?"

"Okay, okay!" It would be her fault if he fell off the horse and broke his neck! Resigned to his fate, he followed Mrs. Minnowpail into the paddock. She took hold of Blackie's halter and smiled encouragingly.

"Up you go!"

"Without a saddle?"

"Yes. That way you'll get a better feel of the horse."

From close up the horse looked even more enormous. "How am I supposed to get on?"

"Just hold on to her mane and swing yourself up."

"Are you sure she'll stand still?" asked Tony nervously.

"Sure. Besides, I'll hold the reins, so don't worry."

"If anything happens, it's on your heads!" called Tony to his parents. Then he took hold of the mane and swung himself up onto the horse's back. It wasn't nearly as hard as he'd expected. Once he was sitting on top, he couldn't help grinning triumphantly.

He pressed his legs tightly against Blackie's flanks and sat up straight, feeling just like a cowboy in a movie. Mrs. Minnowpail watched him.

"Not bad for a beginner," she said. "If you work at it, you'll be riding like a cowboy in no time!"

Tony was flattered. "Do you think so?"

"No doubt about it."

But Tony wasn't so sure she was right, because after an enthusiastic "Giddyap, Blackie!" the horse started to trot. Tony felt as if he were going to bounce right off Blackie's back at every step!

A little later, when he had firm ground under his feet again, he walked stiffly back to his parents.

"You did a great job!" his father praised him.

"Really?"

Mrs. Minnowpail came up to Tony and shook his hand. "You sure did." Turning to Tony's father she added slyly, "And this afternoon we'll see if you can do as well as Tony did."

"Who me?" cried his father.

"And your wife too!" Mrs. Minnowpail responded, laughing.

The nervous looks on his parents' faces made up for everything Tony had been through that morning.

"Right!" he said. "Didn't you hear what Mrs. Minnowpail said: *All* the guests want to ride!"

7 / Jeremy and Joanna

After lunch Tony went to his room. His excuse was that he wanted to read. But he could hardly keep his eyes open. He was worn out from riding and from sneaking Rudolph and his coffin to the farm the night before. He threw himself on the bed and just managed to pull off his boots. Then he was asleep.

Shortly after four his mother knocked on his door. Tony blinked. "What?"

"Dad and I are going riding now."

"I'll be right there," murmured Tony sleepily.

The next thing he heard was his father's voice. "Hey, sleepyhead!"

"I'm . . . coming." Tony opened his eyes and saw his father standing by the bed.

"Do you know how late it is? It's five-thirty!"

"Five-thirty," mumbled Tony in disbelief. He must have gone back to sleep after his mother had knocked. Rats! he thought, he'd slept through his parents' riding lesson and probably missed a few good laughs.

"Did you fall off?" he asked hopefully.

"No."

"Too bad." Tony stretched and yawned.

His father just smiled. "Jeremy and Joanna are back," he said.

Tony groped for his boots and sat up to put them on. "I suppose they want to play with me."

"Jeremy wants to show you the barn. He tells me it has lots of nice, dark places to hide."

Tony was on his feet in an instant. He was positive Rudolph would have hidden his coffin in the barn. If Jeremy and Joanna were planning a game of hide-and-seek, he'd better get to the barn before they found more than they were looking for!

"Sounds like fun, Dad," said Tony as he rushed out of his room.

At the door he nearly ran into Mr. Minnowpail.

"Did you want to see the pigs now?" asked Mr. Minnowpail.

"The pigs? No, I—" Tony stopped. The longer he stood here talking, the more time they'd have to discover the coffin, and he had to make sure that didn't happen at all costs!

"I'll take a look tomorrow!" he called, and ran off before the dazed farmer had a chance to reply.

The door of the barn wasn't latched. It squeaked on its hinges as Tony opened it. Cautiously he took a couple of steps inside and then stopped.

The two small dusty windows near the door hardly let in any light. In the gloom everything looked strange and unreal: the farm implements, the tractor at the far end, the old cart near the wall. A few feet away a rickety ladder led upward. Full of foreboding, Tony studied the narrow rungs. They were old and rotting and the idea of climbing them didn't thrill him at all! Besides, it looked even darker and gloomier at the top than it did down here. Maybe he should just turn around and go back to the farmhouse.

But just then he heard a low giggle, followed by a clear voice that called, "Hey, Tony!"

Startled, he peered up into the murky gloom, but couldn't see anybody.

"Where are you?" he called.

"Come up and find us!" answered the voice.

"Or are you too scared?" added a second.

"I'm not scared!" lied Tony. Knees knocking, he began climbing the wooden ladder. With each step the rungs creaked as if they were going to collapse any second. But at last he reached the top safely.

He looked around uneasily. Bales of hay and straw were piled up everywhere. There were so many, and among them so many hiding places, that he really didn't know where to start looking.

But then he had an idea. Quietly, so as not to give himself away, he found a little hollow in the straw, crept inside—and waited. Tony figured it wouldn't be long before Jeremy and Joanna came out of their hiding places wondering where he was!

And he was right. Before long he heard some excited whispers. Then someone slipped over the straw and stopped very close to his hiding place.

"Can you see him?" a voice whispered.

"No."

"Did he go back down again?"

"How should I know?"

Tony leaned forward cautiously until he could see a pair of tan boots, blue pants, a blue sweatshirt, and the back of a head with short, light brown hair. It was Jeremy.

24

Tony giggled silently.

"I bet he's hiding," said Jeremy.

"Shh. Let's find him," whispered Joanna.

"Okay. Come on."

Tony heard cracking and rustling noises, then footsteps running here and there, and then—silence. Suddenly Joanna was peering into his hiding place.

"Aha! I've got him." She pushed the hay aside. "That was pretty sneaky, waiting till we came out ourselves!"

Tony was delighted that he'd outsmarted them. "I thought I'd surprise you," he said, and stood up. As he brushed the straw from his overalls he looked at Joanna out of the corner of his eye. In her jeans and red boots, and with her blond hair tied back at her neck, she actually looked pretty nice. When she noticed he was looking at her, she began to blush.

"We'd found a *great* place to hide," she said quickly. "Behind an old wooden box."

Tony's heart skipped a beat. Could it be the little vampire's coffin?

"Where is it?" he blurted out.

She pointed into the gloom. "Over there. Near the wall."

The huge box with the old-fashioned lock definitely wasn't Rudolph's. But Tony decided he'd better find out if they knew anything about the vampire's coffin. So he asked, "Are there any other old wooden boxes up here?"

"Why do you want to know?" asked Jeremy.

"Because . . ." Now what was he going to say? He

couldn't think up a good reason, so he said very casually, "Oh, I was just wondering."

"Just wondering!" mimicked Jeremy. "What are you, some kind of treasure hunter?"

"Why don't you tell Tony about the *other* box?" asked Joanna, giggling.

Jeremy threw his sister a furious look. "It's none of his business. And why don't you mind yours, for a change!"

"What kind of box?" asked Tony anxiously.

"A box for his monsters."

"What monsters?" croaked Tony.

"Those gross wiggly ones made out of rubber. Mom wanted to toss them, so Jeremy hid them up here."

"So what!" growled Jeremy. It was obvious he didn't like talking about it, because he changed the subject immediately. "Do you play Ping-Pong?"

"Not very well," said Tony.

"Jeremy can't either," said Joanna. "But I'm really good at it."

"Oh, shut up!" said Jeremy as he started down the ladder.

"I'm better than you!" taunted Joanna.

Tony climbed down after Jeremy. On the one hand he was relieved and glad that the vampire hadn't hidden his coffin in the barn. But on the other hand he didn't have any clues as to where to look next. No matter what happened, he had to find Rudolph before dark!

8 / Shrieks in the Dark

Tony had just won a Ping-Pong game against Jeremy when Mrs. Minnowpail called them to dinner.

"I'll show you my knight collection after we eat," said Jeremy. "We can pretend we're on a quest, looking for damsels in distress."

"Well, maybe," Tony said evasively. "Actually I might have to go to bed," he added with a yawn, even though he wasn't the least bit tired.

"This early?"

"I'm bushed. It must be the country air. . . ."

Jeremy looked disappointed. "What a wimp!"

Normally Tony would have challenged a remark like that, but this time he just smiled.

"I guess I'll just have to play with Joanna," said Jeremy with disgust.

Perfect, thought Tony. Then he'd be able to look for the coffin without the little Minnowpails tagging along. He had to find it before Rudolph flew off!

But Rudolph Sackville-Bagg had hidden his coffin extremely well. Although Tony searched the entire farmyard after dinner, he found no trace of the coffin or Rudolph.

Finally he came to a halt in front of a low cement-block building at the far end of the farmyard. It had no windows and looked like a garage. Cautiously

Tony opened the iron door. In the same instant the most deafening shrieks and cries broke out inside the pitch-dark building. Terrified, he leapt backward, slammed the door, and raced back to the house. Not until he reached the front door did he even dare glance over his shoulder. He was astonished to find there was no hideous monster on his heels. Still shaking, he went inside and climbed the stairs to his room. He sat down on his bed and tried to think. Could it have been an animal? But what kind of animal lived in total darkness and gave out shrieks ten times as hair raising as the peacock?

Then he wondered if the little vampire had anything to do with it. But that didn't make sense. A vampire would *never* make so much noise. Vampires stalked their prey in absolute silence.

And then something awful occurred to him. Suppose the little vampire had opened that same door in his search for a hiding place for his coffin? And suppose the terrible creature inside had grabbed him and pulled him in . . . ? What if Rudolph was trapped in there right now, hoping desperately that Tony would come and rescue him?

Tony decided to go downstairs and ask Joanna exactly what the building was used for and what could have made those horrible shrieks.

Joanna was sprawled in front of the TV—watching a wrestling match, Tony noticed with surprise.

"Excuse me, I have to ask you something," he said.

"Not now," she replied. "Wait till this is over. It's the championship."

Tony groaned softly. He couldn't even wait until the next commercial if he was going to be in time to help the vampire.

"I can't," he said urgently. "I've got to know right now what's in that cement-block building at the far end of the farmyard. Just a few minutes ago, when I opened the door—"

"You opened the door?" interrupted Joanna, chuckling. "I bet I know what happened next!"

"Do you know what's inside?"

"Don't you?" she asked. "Didn't you hear the squealing?" she added with a giggle.

"Squealing?" Suddenly it dawned on Tony. "The pigs?"

"What did you think they were? Monsters?"

Tony's cheeks were burning. Scared by a bunch of pigs! he thought disgustedly. But wait a minute: Pigsties weren't supposed to look like that. And pigs didn't live in the dark.

"I don't believe you!" he said boldly. "Pigsties have windows!"

"But it isn't a regular pigsty," explained Joanna. "We keep pigs for fattening."

"And they have to live in the dark?"

"Yes. They only see daylight when Dad goes in to turn on the automatic feeders. That's why they squealed like that when you opened the door."

"But that's—that's cruelty to animals!" said Tony heatedly.

Joanna shrugged her shoulders. "My father says it helps the pigs to fatten up faster, and it saves him a lot of time. He doesn't even have to clean them out anymore. Everything gets done automatically."

"It's still torture!"

"Well, they weren't much better off in the old pigsty. Take a look for yourself, if you don't believe me. It's just full of junk now."

Tony pricked up his ears. An old pigsty full of junk? Could the little vampire have chosen that as his hiding place?

"Where exactly is it?" asked Tony, trying to hide his excitement.

"Out behind the cow shed. Can't we talk about this later? I *really* want to see the end of this fight."

And I really want to take a look at that old pigsty, thought Tony. "Okay, see you later," he said as he headed for the front door.

9 / Vampire Teeth

In the meantime night had fallen. It never got this dark at home in the city, thought Tony with a shudder. The moon had vanished behind some clouds, and the glow from the streetlights shimmered only faintly through the tall trees at the edge of the road. His pocket flashlight would have come in really handy right now. But he'd completely forgotten it in his frenzy to get the vampire's spare cape packed this morning. Typical dumb move! he thought disgustedly.

When he finally reached the back of the cow shed, he took a deep breath in spite of the horrible stench. For there behind the manure heap he could make out the roof of a shed. It must be the old pigsty!

As he carefully made his way around the manure heap, he saw that the shed was made of brick, with small windows and a wooden door. And the door was half open . . . !

Tony froze, his heart beating wildly. Wasn't that a light at the window? And wasn't that a strange shadow that slipped out around the door? He shivered. Suppose it *wasn't* the little vampire? What if it was Aunt Dorothy, or some other vampire, one from around here . . . ?

And in the dark silence around him he suddenly heard a noise: It was a clear, clicking sound, the sound of needle-sharp teeth biting together! Vampire teeth!

Without thinking, Tony took a couple of steps backward—and came to a halt with one boot stuck firmly in the mucky ground. "Rats!" he whispered quietly through tight lips. No matter how he twisted and pulled, his boot wouldn't budge! This would have to happen now, when over by the pigsty there might be a vampire lying in wait for him!

Rigid with fright, Tony saw a figure detach itself from the darkness of the doorway and glide silently and stealthily toward him. Its full-length cape swelled out around it, so that it looked like some gigantic black bat.

Just then the moon came out from behind the clouds and Tony found himself looking at the deathly pale face of the little vampire!

"Rudolph!" he cried, his voice quivering with relief. "Boy, am I glad to see you!"

"Hello, Tony," said the vampire gloomily.

Tony noticed Rudolph's red-rimmed eyes and large mouth, with its widely spaced canine teeth, as sharp as needles. At the sight of those vampire teeth a shiver ran down his spine. . . .

"I—I was coming to visit you," he said quickly.

"Visit me?" Rudolph laughed hoarsely. "What a good idea! I can't tell you how hungry I am!"

"I didn't mean it like that!"

"How did you mean it, then?" The vampire took a step nearer Tony.

Tony tried to back away, but his boot was still firmly stuck in the mud. Cold sweat broke out on his

forehead. But he didn't dare let the vampire realize how frightened he was.

"I just wanted to find out where you had put your coffin," he said evenly.

"My coffin?" The vampire's face took on a distrustful look. "Why?"

There was only one answer to that!

"We're friends, aren't we?" said Tony, putting all his powers of persuasion into the words.

Rudolph tightened his lips and growled, "Friends! I'm too *hungry* to think about friends!" And he cast a longing glance at Tony's neck.

"Didn't I help you bring that heavy coffin all the way here?" asked Tony.

"Yes," hissed the vampire.

"And I even paid for the train tickets out of my own money!"

Rudolph looked at Tony testily. "You're making it sound as if you did it all just to please me!"

"Didn't I?" cried Tony.

"You wanted me to come so you wouldn't be completely bored stuck on a farm in the middle of nowhere! That's how you talked me into coming with you!"

Tony had to smile. That was quite true—but the vampire also had his own good reasons for leaving the family vault for a couple of days!

"And what about George the Boisterous?" he retorted. "Didn't Gruesome Gregory invite him to stay in your vault? And didn't George say he was going to pulverize you?"

35

"Well, yes," admitted the vampire. "But I'm sure I wouldn't have chosen this lousy farm as a hideout," he added fiercely. "I absolutely cannot find a decent meal here. Yesterday I was out on the prowl for half the night, and all I could catch was a mouse!"

"You just haven't found your way around yet," said Tony. "I bet you don't even know where the bulls are!"

"Bulls . . . that's all I need!" said the vampire grumpily.

"And the chickens!" continued Tony. "I can show you where the chicken coop is! And I even know where there's a la—" He was going to say "lamb," but he hesitated as he thought of the cuddly little white bundle.

"What's a la—?" spit the vampire.

But Tony had decided not to tell him about the lamb. "Laying hens!" he said instead.

"Laying hens!" echoed the vampire. "Just shut up about all those animals, will you!"

Tony held his breath and gave another tug at his boot—and this time managed to get it free. With a sigh of relief he said, "Can I have a quick look?"

"A quick look at what?" asked the vampire suspiciously.

"At the pigsty. Or haven't you unpacked yet?" asked Tony with a giggle.

"Yes, I have. But hurry up! I'm so hungry, I could eat a horse!"

10 / The Little Vampire's Hideout

Tony slipped through the door of the pigsty behind the little vampire. They came into the first part, which was stacked high with old furniture. By the wall stood an old wardrobe with a long mirror on its door. In the dim light that came from the main part of the pigsty, Tony could see his reflection. But where the vampire should have been, the mirror was empty!

He spun around—and there was the vampire, large as life, with his tousled hair hanging to his shoulders, and his grubby cape with its moth holes. Tony gulped. He knew very well that a vampire's image doesn't reflect in a mirror. But there was a big difference between reading about it in a book and actually finding it was true in real life. But then he giggled. After all, this wasn't just any old vampire, it was Rudolph Sackville-Bagg, his best friend. There was no reason to be scared of him—was there?

All the same he felt a little nervous as he followed the vampire into a long room with waist-high brick partitions for the pigs. Everywhere there were planks of wood, furniture, tools, rolls of wire, and iron stakes. The thick layer of dust over everything showed that hardly anyone ever ventured inside. On top of all that it stank unbelievably of pig manure and mildew. But it was the perfect hideout for the vampire.

His little black coffin, hidden in a corner between

a worm-eaten barrel and a large chest, wouldn't have been noticeable at all amid all the clutter—except that there was a candle burning on the edge of it. Tony knew Rudolph needed the candle to read a little when he woke up—vampire stories, of course!

"What a terrific hiding place!" he said approvingly.

The vampire gave a pleased smile. "It is, isn't it? How did you manage to find me?"

Tony made a sweeping gesture. "I looked everywhere! Finally Joanna told me about this old pigsty."

"Joanna?" asked the vampire suspiciously. "Who's she? Does she know anything?"

Tony cleared his throat in embarrassment. "She lives here on the farm. But she doesn't know a thing about you. Anyway, she doesn't believe in vampires," he added, even though he didn't know if that was true, "so you're totally safe."

That seemed to calm the vampire. He pulled out a hat and put it on. Tony had to bite his lips to keep from laughing out loud. It was the Tyrolean hat that he'd lent the vampire as a disguise for the train trip to the farm! With the hat on his head, its long feather whipping up and down with every movement, the little vampire really looked pretty silly!

But evidently Rudolph thought he looked very dashing, for he was smiling proudly.

"Shall we go?" he said.

"Where?"

"You were going to show me where I could get something to eat!"

11 / Chicken Eyes

As they left the pigsty the vampire asked, "All right, where are the bulls?"

"The b-bulls?" Tony wasn't exactly sure where the bulls' pasture was. And the thought of meeting a bull in a dark pasture didn't thrill him in the least. "What about going to the chicken coop first?"

"Chickens!" said the vampire scornfully. "They're nothing but bones and feathers. I'd never get full on that!"

"But there are plenty of them," countered Tony.

"Grrr!" was all the vampire said.

"The bulls are pretty fierce," tried Tony.

"Fierce?" The little vampire didn't sound quite so sure of himself now. "Do you mean, they might . . . do something to me?"

"Well, they—"

"Okay, let's go to the chicken coop first," agreed the vampire hastily.

Tony grinned to himself. The little vampire always acted as if he were totally courageous and unafraid, but in fact, he was just as easily scared as Tony!

Would Rudolph be frightened of the chickens? Tony had already made up his mind never to go near them again himself. He would stand by the fence and watch them all tweaking at the vampire's holey old stockings! At the thought of the vampire, cape flapping, running around among all those pecking beaks, Tony gave a soft chuckle.

But he stopped laughing as soon as he reached the fence. There wasn't a single chicken in sight!

"So where are all these chickens of yours?" growled the vampire with obvious disappointment.

"Well—they, uh . . ." Tony began. He'd expected to see them clucking and pecking on the other side of the fence. "They, uh, must be asleep."

"Where?" asked the vampire, clicking his teeth.

Of course, Tony couldn't admit that he had absolutely no idea where they were. He pointed uncertainly to the coop inside the fence. "They must be in there."

"All of them?" asked the vampire in disbelief. "I thought you said there were plenty of them?"

"Well, some of them go to roost in the trees."

"Chickens? In trees?"

"Why not? They're birds, aren't they?"

"Vampires may not know much about wildlife," declared the vampire, "but chickens in trees—I've never heard of that before!"

Neither have I, Tony secretly had to agree with him. Aloud he said, "Can't you see their eyes?"

The vampire obviously didn't know what chicken eyes looked like, because he became very serious, and his sharp eyes, which could see much better in the dark than Tony's, peered up into the tops of the trees.

"There is something up there," he said. "I can't see any eyes, but I can see a shadow moving."

"A shadow moving?" cried Tony in alarm. After

41

all, he'd only made it up about chickens roosting in trees! "Is it an animal?" he asked anxiously.

"Maybe it's a vampire!" said Rudolph with a broad grin.

"A v-vampire?" Tony's voice was shaking.

Rudolph gave him an amused glance. "Since when have you been afraid of vampires?"

"I—uh—it might be Aunt Dorothy."

"Impossible. She's much fatter than that."

"Or Sabina the Sinister?"

"My grandmother certainly doesn't go around lurking in treetops," retorted the vampire haughtily. "But it might be my sister, Anna."

"Anna? What would she be doing here?"

"She just always wants to be where you are!" responded the vampire with a cackle.

Tony felt himself blushing. "Oh, shut up!"

The vampire cackled again, and recited:

"Lovesick old Anna, perched high in a tree,
Twittering just like a starling.
Down on the ground her boyfriend gazed up,
And wished he were next to his darling!"

"Very funny!" said Tony furiously. To pay the vampire back he said, "I bet it's McRookery!" He knew how frightened the vampires were of the night watchman at the cemetery who was constantly on their trail and had vowed to get rid of every single one of them. He'd already done in Rudolph's uncle Theodore.

But the little vampire was unruffled. "And since when has McRookery been able to fly?"

Now Tony could see the mysterious creature for himself. Slowly and clumsily it flew down from the tree. As it perched on the chain-link fence and gave a harsh and piercing cry, he suddenly knew what it was. . . .

But it was too late to tell the little vampire, for in the same instant he had taken to his heels and fled.

"Oh, well," said Tony, going back to the farmhouse. "So I forgot to warn him about the peacock. Serves him right for making up that stupid poem!"

12 / Country People

The next morning Tony's parents insisted that he go for a walk with them, even though it was the last thing he felt like doing.

"Otherwise you'll just sit in your room!" declared his mother.

"Or mope around the farm getting bored," added his father.

"Going for a walk isn't exactly mind-blowing!" retorted Tony.

"Sure it is," said his father. "There'll be all kinds of interesting things to look at."

Tony pointed to a couple of bags of trash that were sitting by the side of the road. "You mean, like those?"

"You know perfectly well what your father means," said his mother, giving him one of her not-another-word looks.

Tony was silent, irritated. Why did *they* always get to decide what was good for him!

Moodily he followed along behind them and tried not to listen to their conversation about old farmhouses, leaded windows, and farmhouse curtains—which wasn't exactly easy because they chattered enthusiastically about every "object of interest" they saw.

Just like tourists! thought Tony disdainfully.

When they began oohing and aahing over a three-foot-high windmill in someone's garden, and its owners looked curiously over at them, Tony felt his face turn beet-red.

"Do you have to talk so loudly?" he hissed.

Ignoring him, his parents began to question the people about their house, the windmill, and any other "objects of interest" to be found in Lower Bogsbottom. Tony crossed to the other side of the road and pretended he didn't even know them. When he had counted to twenty-five his parents came over to him.

"Country people are so open and friendly!" his mother was saying.

"Unlike joyboy here," his father chimed in with a glance at Tony's stormy expression.

"At home you don't go around talking to every other person on the street!" he growled. "You're acting like real tourists!"

His mother just laughed. "Right! And now, like real tourists, we're going to take a look at the church!"

"That's all I need!" muttered Tony.

Then it occurred to him that if there was a church, then it must have a graveyard to explore—and that thought made him feel better.

But it was a recent graveyard, as Tony soon discovered to his disappointment. It was surrounded by a low stone wall, and its paths were perfectly straight and neatly raked; it had only a few bushes and trees. The gravestones stood in such immaculate rows, and the graves were so carefully tended, it made him yawn. There certainly weren't any vampire graves in this cemetery—or were there? In the last row he found this epitaph:

45

BURIED DEEP
IN TIMELESS SLEEP
LIES OUR EARTHLY CORE;
WHAT WE LOVED
LIVES ON ABOVE
AND FOREVERMORE.

But the grave was much too well cared for to be
a vampire's grave! Vampire graves, as far as Tony
knew, had ancient weathered gravestones and were
overgrown with weeds.

"Well, did you discover any vampires' graves?"
asked his father when they all met in front of the
church.

"I sure did!" said Tony, bristling at his father's
teasing tone of voice. "The whole cemetery is full of
them. And there's a vampire running around with a
shovel and a wheelbarrow, trying to dig himself a
grave. If you hurry up, you'll catch him before he
buries himself."

"Now, what made me think that vampires only
came out at night?" remarked his father in an amused
tone.

Tony threw him a grim look and growled, "Thank
you, Mr. Know-it-all!"

"Can't you both talk about something else?" interrupted his mother heatedly. "What about those nice
old houses, for instance?"

"They really *are* pretty," agreed his father. "Just
look at that one with the balcony. . . ."

Here we go again! thought Tony, grumpily following along behind them.

He stayed in a bad mood until they stopped on the way back at a shop with a sign that said GOLDIE GRAPPLE'S GROCERIES. It sure doesn't *look* like a grocery store, thought Tony. There were no SALE signs or even anything on display in the windows; they were simply half covered over with butcher's paper.

"Some grocery store!" he said, grinning.

"They're always like this in the country," said his mother. "Come on, let's go in."

"Okay," said Tony quickly. If it really was a grocery store, it was bound to have cookies and candy. And all he'd had to eat that day was half a roll. But they were hardly inside before Tony's mother, noticing a long shelf with jars full of candy, said, "But we're not buying any of that!"

"Why not?" asked Tony.

"Because you didn't eat a proper breakfast."

"Aw, Mom!" he groaned. They even had his favorite kind of chocolate here—his mouth watered when he saw it. "I promise I'll eat a proper lunch, and dinner too."

But his mother shook her head. "No, absolutely not!"

"I need chocolate!" Tony said obstinately.

"Have a piece of fudge," said the woman behind the cash register.

Tony's mother opened her mouth to protest, but then closed it again. She probably didn't want to seem rude. But Tony could tell from the look on her face that she was furious at the saleswoman for interfering with the way she was dealing with her son.

He took the fudge with a grin, and quickly popped it into his mouth. "You were right," he remarked to his mother innocently. "Country people *are* really nice!" He wandered happily around the shop. You could buy practically anything, from broomsticks to baked beans. He even found some books. But none of them interested him. His mother, on the other hand, went on and on about them.

"Tony, look at all these wonderful books! Animal stories! Craft books! Adventure stories! Fairy tales! Myths! Would you like me to buy one for you?"

"No thanks."

"But then you could spend the afternoon reading."

I can do that anyway, thought Tony. Aloud he said, "Those are just for farm kids."

"What do you like to read?" inquired the saleswoman.

Just to torment his mother Tony said, "Vampire stories!"

To his surprise the woman didn't laugh at his reply. Instead she stepped out from behind the counter and took a few books down from a shelf—books with black covers, he noticed eagerly.

"Here," she said, handing Tony three books. "Will these do?"

They were vampire stories! Tony had already read two of them, but the third, with the promising title *The Bloodless Corpse,* was new to him.

He turned to his mother and asked, "Will you buy this one for me?"

"I certainly will not!" she answered crossly.

"It's not quite as gory as it sounds," said the saleswoman. "My children really loved it!"

"See?" said Tony triumphantly. "Country people know how to pick good books!"

The saleswoman looked flattered and smiled, but she didn't offer to give him the book, which was what he had hoped would happen. So he had to pay for it out of his own money. But Tony didn't really mind. He had a brand-new vampire book to show for it, and now he knew exactly how he was going to spend the afternoon!

13 / The Little Vampire and the Monsters

When Tony went into the old pigsty that evening, the vampire was still in his coffin. The candle was burning, but the vampire wasn't reading as he usually did. He'd pulled his moth-eaten black blanket right up to his chin, and he stared at Tony with bloodshot eyes.

"Don't you feel well?" asked Tony.

The vampire pulled the blanket down so that Tony could see a small scratch on his neck.

"I'm wounded!"

Tony nearly laughed out loud—the scratch didn't look all *that* bad!

With a look of great suffering the vampire said, "I'm sure I'm going to get blood poisoning. Greg had it once. He almost died of it!"

"But vampires are already dead," remarked Tony.

The vampire threw him a furious look, as he always did when Tony caught him exaggerating.

"So what?" he hissed. "We can still get blood poisoning!" He touched the scratch gingerly. "Is it very deep?"

"No," said Tony reassuringly.

"If only I could see it! I can't look at it in a mirror. . . . Did you see a red mark on my neck? Greg said if you get blood poisoning, you get a red mark too."

Tony did his best not to laugh. The only mark the vampire had on his neck was a black one—and that was dirt! But he thought he'd better not say that out loud. "You look pretty normal to me," he declared. And he was right. The vampire looked just as pale and grubby as he always did. Only, the rings under his eyes might have been a little darker than usual.

"Normal!" retorted the vampire. "After a night like that I couldn't possibly look normal!"

"What in the world happened?" asked Tony eagerly.

The vampire looked at him with glittering eyes. "The farmyard is full of monsters!"

"Monsters?" Tony tried to keep a straight face. He knew only too well what kind of monsters the vampire had bumped into! "If you mean that thing that gave the awful cry . . ."

But before Tony could explain that it was only the

peacock they had seen, the little vampire interrupted him. "That was nothing!" he cried. "Later, while I was crossing the field, a monster came charging up to me—it was bigger than a house—and it hit me!"

Tony quickly put his hand over his mouth. It must have been one of the horses! "Is that how you got the scratch?"

"The what?" asked the vampire, looking hurt.

"The—uh—the wound, on your neck," Tony corrected himself. "Did the monster do it to you?"

"No," said the vampire in a sepulchral voice. "Another monster came galloping up to me. So with my last ounce of strength I jumped into some bushes."

"And so your neck got scratched on the thorns?"

The vampire closed his eyes, as if the memory caused him great pain. "No," he said slowly. "There was a third monster in the bushes."

Tony gulped to keep from laughing. "Not another one?"

"Yes! It must have been lying in wait for me, because it immediately jumped on me and bit me in the neck. I fainted."

"How awful!" said Tony. It was probably best if he went along with this story of a monster in the bushes, even though he was sure the vampire had simply scratched himself on the thorns! With a straight face he said, "Gosh, it must have been a vampire!"

"What do you mean?"

"Because it bit you on the neck."

The vampire looked indignant. "Vampires don't bite one another. No, it was definitely a monster!"

52

Tony had to smile at the horror in Rudolph's voice as he said the word *monster*. There was only one monster here on the farm—and that was the little vampire himself!

"But I'm going to find out what kind of monster it was!" With these words the vampire stood up and climbed out of his coffin.

"Now?" asked Tony excitedly. To go with Rudolph on a monster hunt would be really exciting.

"No. First I need something to eat."

As usual Tony shuddered at the thought of the vampire's eating habits. Even so, he asked bravely, "Can I go with you?" He could always look away when the vampire actually bit his prey. "I promise I'll be totally quiet."

The vampire shook his head. "No. You'd only be in the way."

"I wouldn't," Tony assured him enthusiastically.

"Why are you so eager to come along?" asked the vampire reluctantly.

"Why?" Tony took a deep breath. "If you only knew how bored I've been today! All I've done the whole day is go for a walk with my parents, read, eat . . ."

The vampire looked at Tony sympathetically.

"All I've thought about all day is the fun we could have tonight," continued Tony persuasively.

"And what if I need to fly?" growled the vampire.

Tony had been waiting for that question. With a beaming smile he pulled out the spare cape from under his sweatshirt. "See? I planned ahead!"

At the sight of the cape the vampire grinned. "Okay, then," he said. "You can come with me. But don't try to get mixed up in my—business!"

"Okay. I promise." Tony was only too glad to agree. Once outside he asked, "Where's your hat, by the way?"

"It's gone," said the vampire gloomily.

"Gone?" That startled Tony. He couldn't have cared less what happened to his Tyrolean hat, but his parents would be furious. "How did that happen?"

"I lost it when the first monster attacked me."

"Then it must still be in the field," said Tony in a relieved voice. "Come on. Let's go find it."

Rudolph gave a cry of horror. "Go after those monsters on an empty stomach? Never!" And afraid Tony might object, he took off into the air.

"Wait!" called Tony.

He quickly put on the cape, which smelled of musty coffins. It was made of black material, practically worn out, and full of moth holes. With a pounding heart Tony stretched out his arms and moved them cautiously up and down, and at once he began to float. He gave a few vigorous flaps—and away he flew.

Soon the farmyard below looked like a model in a toy store. Tony thought of his parents, of Joanna and Jeremy, of Mrs. Minnowpail and her husband, all sitting in the farmhouse without the least idea that here he was, flying through the night sky—and suddenly he had to laugh out loud.

"Have you gone crazy?" hissed the vampire furiously. "Do you want someone to hear us?"

"No one's going to hear us up here," Tony said defensively.

"You think so?" spit the vampire venomously. "And what if Aunt Dorothy just happened to be flying past?"

Tony gasped. "Can you see her somewhere?"

"No. But you never know," replied the vampire. "Now, hurry up—before I die of hunger!"

14 / What a Courageous Vampire!

"Where are we going?" asked Tony.

The vampire pointed to the dome of a church in the distance, which looked sort of like an onion.

"To Oniontown," he said, and added fervently, "I hope there won't be any monsters there!"

I'm sure there won't be, thought Tony, but there will be people!

That afternoon he'd made up a song, and it seemed to fit the occasion now. So as they flitted through the night together he began to sing softly:

> *"When Rudolph reached his hundredth year*
> *A present came from Grandma dear:*
> *A black wool cape with magic power*
> *To help him fly and soar and tower—*
> *Now he was a true vampire!"*

"What are you singing?" asked the vampire. "Are you singing about me?"

Tony grinned. "Maybe."

"Sing it again!" demanded the vampire.

"Only if you promise to be nice," said Tony, and he began to sing while the vampire listened attentively.

> *"Out of the vault did Rudolph fly*
> *And winged his way through the dark night sky.*

The air was cold, and down below
The woods seemed just the place to go.

"But in the woods he met a bear.
It gave poor Rudolph quite a scare!
Back to the town he turned and flew
But Rudolph's luck ran out there too.

"A thousand streetlights burning bright
Made sure the town was full of light.
'Let's catch him quickly!' came the cry
As lots of people saw him fly.

"Chased by the crowd with nets and sticks
Poor Rudolph was in quite a fix.
Frightened and scared, he found a hole—
He's still there now, for all I know!"

"Not bad!" said the vampire when Tony had finished. "Except it's not true to life."

"What do you mean?" asked Tony heatedly. He thought he'd managed to portray the vampire in his song exactly as he was in real life.

"No vampire would ever crawl into a hole," explained the little vampire. "And vampires don't get scared either. I'd sing it like this:

"Brave Rudolph was no scaredy-cat—
He bit them all, and that was that!"

He ended his version with a grating cackle.

Tony just clamped his mouth shut knowingly. Soon they'd see just how brave the vampire really was, be-

58

cause already the first houses of the little town were coming into view.

With a grin Tony pointed to a brightly lit house with its front door standing wide open. Several well-dressed people were going inside.

"If you're so brave," he said, "here's your chance to prove it!"

"What do you mean?"

"It looks like there's a fancy party going on down there."

"So what? I don't want to dance."

"You don't have to dance!" Tony tried not to laugh. "But think of all those people. It's just what you've been looking for."

Just then a taxi pulled up in front of the house and two men got out.

"Don't they look appetizing?" asked Tony. "After all, you're so courageous," he added sarcastically.

"I'm not *thaaat* courageous," said the little vampire plaintively. The thought of facing so many people had made him even paler than usual. "I'd—I'd rather find a quieter spot," he murmured as he turned away and flew speedily off in another direction.

Tony followed him, singing softly:

> *"Courageous Rudolph found a hole—*
> *He's still there now, for all I know!"*

15 / Seeing into the Future

At first Tony thought the little vampire was going to fly back to the farm, because he was retracing the same route they'd flown to Oniontown. But then he turned right at a sign that said WEST BATSTEEPLE— 2 MILES. When a small farmhouse came into view, he slowed down, turned to Tony, and pointed. The farm- house stood among tall trees. Above the blue front door an old-fashioned porch light was burning, and two of the windows on the ground floor were lit up.

"Now, this is my kind of place!" said the vampire eagerly. "I bet there's an old couple living here with their six grandchildren. The children are already in bed and the old folks are just about to go to sleep. The children's parents were probably killed in a plane crash," he added in a whisper.

Tony was astounded by the little vampire's fertile imagination.

"In the stables out back they keep cows and horses and lambs . . ." As he listed the animals the vampire's voice took on such a longing, hungry tone that Tony began to shudder. "Of course, they've locked the front door," the vampire continued excitedly. "Old people are very careful. But I bet they've forgotten to bolt the back door. Old people are forgetful too." He broke out into a hoarse laugh and landed in the shadow of a tall tree. "Hurry up, Tony!"

"Why don't you go on alone? I'd probably just be in the way, like you said."

"No. You know your way around houses much better than I do."

"But I don't know anything about farmhouses."

"You just want to get out of it!"

"I do not!" contradicted Tony.

"Well, then," said the vampire, grinning, "let's just go and see if the back door is open."

Tony looked over at the house. With its bright curtains, cheery window boxes, and blue front door, it really didn't look all that forbidding. It looked as if kindly, harmless people lived there.

"Well, okay," he said, "if you go first."

"Fine," grunted the vampire.

Slowly and carefully he made his way toward the house and opened the little wrought-iron gate that led to the garden.

"Come on!" he hissed to Tony.

Tony followed on tiptoe, but he wasn't able to move as silently as the vampire. At each step twigs snapped and gravel crunched under his feet—or a bird would suddenly fly up in front of him with a startled chirp. At every sound the vampire turned and glared at him.

Luckily no one in the house seemed aware of them, for the windows facing the garden remained dark.

At last they came to a brick patio with a round table, four chairs, and a barbecue.

"Go and see if the back door is open!" commanded the vampire.

"Why me?" protested Tony.

"Because I've got better eyes and have to stand guard here," replied the vampire—not very convincingly, thought Tony. Nevertheless, with knees knocking, he walked over to the door and hesitantly tried the handle. The door was locked!

Rudolph cracked his knuckles nervously. "Then we'll have to try the front," he said, and added pompously, "They must have gotten confused about the doors. I bet it's the front they've forgotten to lock."

"Maybe you should take up seeing into the future!" Tony said sarcastically.

But instead of being offended, the vampire just smiled. In a strangely lulling tone of voice he said, "Oh, no, not me. You're the one who's going to see into the future."

"What do you mean?" asked Tony suspiciously.

The vampire grinned. "All you have to do is go to the front door, open it, and see what the future holds in store for us!"

For a second Tony was speechless. Then he exclaimed, "If that isn't just like you! You *always* make me go first, just because you're a coward!"

"What did you call me? A coward?" The vampire's voice crackled with rage. "No one has ever—"

He got no further, because just then a light went on in the room facing the patio. The door opened, and a young woman in a long nightgown came out.

"I'm so glad you're finally here!" she cried, and her voice sounded friendly and excited.

16 / Two Visitors from the Orphanage

Tony and the little vampire were so surprised that they stood motionless as if struck by lightning—even when a tall, broad-shouldered man in a blue dressing-gown appeared behind her.

"Our vacation guests are here!" the woman cried. "It's Bernard and Roger from the orphanage!"

"We wondered what happened to you," the man replied in a rumbling voice. "Did you miss your train?"

Tony thought quickly. Obviously the man and the woman were expecting two children from an orphanage to spend their vacation with them who, for some reason, had been delayed. And so they thought Tony and Rudolph were their little orphans! What a lucky break, thought Tony. All they had to do was pretend they were the children, and wait for the first available opportunity to disappear!

"We got on the wrong train by mistake!" he said bravely.

"The wrong train?" asked the woman. "But didn't someone from the orphanage see you off?"

"Uh, yes," said Tony, "but she put us on the wrong one." He added with a grin, "You see, she didn't have her glasses on!"

The woman shook her head in disbelief. "When did you first notice?"

"That she didn't have her glasses on?"

"That you were on the wrong train!"

Before Tony could think of an answer to this, the man said, "Well, never mind. We're very glad you're here now, and we hope this four-week vacation will be lots of fun for you."

"Four weeks!" cried the vampire in horror.

The man laughed. "I don't think four weeks will be long enough for you, you look so pale!"

"My friend needs a little time to get used to country air," said Tony quickly. "He's a real city kid."

"Your friend?" said the woman in surprise. "But the letters from the orphanage said that you were brothers!"

"Right, uh, half-brothers," said Tony.

He had the feeling that the whole thing was becoming pretty risky. Besides, the little vampire had a look on his face as if he was about to take to his heels, and if he did that, the man and the woman were sure to become suspicious. And what might happen after that, Tony didn't want to think about!

He said quickly, "We'd better get our luggage. Come on, Roger."

The vampire looked at Tony blankly. "What luggage?" he grumbled.

Tony tried to stay calm, even though his heart was beating furiously. "Our suitcases! You know!" As he spoke, he stared entreatingly at the vampire. Finally it dawned on Rudolph.

"Oh, right," he said, winking at Tony. "Our suitcases!"

Tony gave a sigh of relief.

"Your suitcases?" repeated the man in astonishment. "Aren't they at the station?"

"They—they're back there," said Tony, pointing in the direction they had come from. "We left them, uh, just up the road. Come on, Roger!" he urged the vampire.

"Wait a minute," said the man, "I'll come with you. Just let me go and put on some clothes." With that he went into the house.

Tony held his breath. This was the moment he had been waiting for.

"We'll go on ahead," he said to the woman. Then he grabbed the vampire's arm and they disappeared into the bushes and shrubs. As soon as they were out of sight, they spread their cloaks and flew.

Once aloft the whole adventure seemed hysterically funny to Tony. "Can't you just see tomorrow's headline in the *West Batsteeple Gazette*," he said, laughing. "Mystery orphans disappear into thin air. Were they extraterrestrials?"

But the vampire wasn't in the mood for jokes. Scowling, he flew to the sign that read: WEST BATSTEEPLE—2 MILES. Perching on it, he declared, "From now on I'll go on alone."

"Why?" asked Tony in surprise as he tried to hover in the air over the sign.

"With you around all I run into is bad luck!" said the vampire.

"What!" Tony was outraged. "And who practically saved your life just now?"

"Hah!" Rudolph snorted contemptuously. "You were the one who lured me to that farmhouse in the first place!"

"I lured you?" said Tony flabbergasted. "And who said, 'This is my kind of place'?"

In his most ghostly voice the vampire said, "You did."

"Me?" croaked Tony.

"Yes, you!" exclaimed the vampire. "If you hadn't made up all that stuff about old people who always forget to lock their back doors, I would have flown on!"

Tony gasped for air. "Oh, sure! Mr. Perfect Sack-ville-Bagg," he yelled. "Nothing is *ever* your fault. You—you—egomaniac!"

The vampire's face lit up. "Egomaniac! Oh, I like the way that sounds. Is it something wicked?"

Tony did not reply.

"It has to be something wicked," said the vampire happily. "Just wait till I tell Greg and Aunt Dorothy that someone called me an egomaniac!"

"Then you can also tell them that you're the nastiest, most ungrateful creep I have ever met!" cried Tony. "You make me sick!"

He turned sharply in the air. As he flew away, he could see the vampire, still crouching on the signpost, with a self-satisfied smile on his face.

17 / Vampires? No Thanks!

Tony spent the following morning in bed. He told his parents he had a stomachache. It wasn't exactly true, but after his argument with the vampire and the lonely flight home, he needed a little rest.

He took *Vampire Stories for Advanced Readers* out of the closet where he'd hidden it and turned to one of his favorite stories: "The Bats." It was about a boy who kept bats in an old shed. He was trying to tame them. And two little puncture marks on his neck betrayed how he managed to do it. . . .

The story had always given Tony a pleasant case of the shivers whenever he read it. But today he was surprised to find that it only made him feel a sudden aversion to bats. Could it have something to do with his anger with Rudolph?

Determined not to think about the vampire, he snapped the book shut. Then he inspected the books on the little shelf above Joanna's bed. *My Pony and Me; Me and My Pony; The Old Man and the Pony; The Old Woman and the Pony; The Gray Gelding Returns*. After a short hesitation he took out *Born to Gallop*. The back cover said it was about the theft of a pony. He threw himself on the bed again and began to read.

That afternoon, when he met Joanna and Jeremy in front of the barn, he said to Joanna, "You know, some of your books aren't too bad!"

"Do you think so?" She was pleased.

"*Born to Gallop* is really very exciting."

"I thought you only liked vampire books."

Tony stuffed his hands into his pockets. "Vampires? No thanks!" he declared, so loudly that even the little vampire in his coffin might have heard him.

"But don't you have a friend who's a vampire?"

"Who told you that?"

"My mom."

"How would she know?" asked Tony scornfully.

"Isn't it true?" asked Jeremy nosily.

"Do you believe in vampires?" replied Tony.

"No."

"Well, then."

Joanna was more stubborn. "Have you got a friend who's a vampire, or not?"

"I haven't got a *friend* who's a vampire," answered Tony, and that was the truth. Rudolph Sackville-Bagg might be a vampire, but he certainly wasn't his friend anymore!

"If you're tired of your vampires, why don't we play with my knights?" suggested Jeremy.

Why not? thought Tony. Perhaps playing with knights wouldn't be so boring after all. Besides, it would keep him from thinking about that conceited, bossy, ungrateful little vampire! Rudolph Sackville-Bagg could just wait and see how Tony got on without him. "Okay," said Tony. "And let's play together after dinner too," he added. "I don't have anything else to do."

18 / Funny Business with the Eggs

The next morning Tony was the first one down to the breakfast table.

"You're up already?" said his father in astonishment, when he came down ten minutes later.

"Well, sure," said Tony, embarrassed. "Why shouldn't I be?"

Naturally, he wasn't about to tell his father that he had quarreled with the little vampire and had gone to bed at nine o'clock after spending two boring hours with Jeremy and his knights. Knights just weren't the same as vampires!

"Isn't Mom up yet?" he asked.

"No. She hardly slept a wink last night."

Just then the two other guests at the farmhouse came in. Up till now Tony had carefully avoided meeting them, because they were the same two ladies he and Rudolph had seen on the train trip to Lower Bogsbottom. He peered anxiously over at them now, but they barely noticed him.

The smaller of the two turned to Tony's father and said excitedly, "Couldn't your wife sleep either? We've been here since Saturday and haven't had a good night's sleep yet!"

"Because of all the awful noises," added the larger lady.

"What noises?" asked Tony's father.

"Terrible cries! As if somebody were being strangled!" answered the larger lady.

"And then there are those giant moths fluttering around the house," continued the smaller one. "Yesterday, when we couldn't sleep, we were going to open a window, and outside we saw a moth as big as a child! It was squatting on the windowsill staring at us. Oh, I will *never* forget those horrible red eyes as long as I live!"

Tony's father smiled slyly. "Too bad my son didn't see it."

"Why?" cried Tony, worried that his father's comment might have directed the ladies' attention to him.

"Well, it sounds like a vampire, doesn't it?"

The two ladies exchanged looks.

"Are there vampires around here?" the smaller one asked nervously.

"Of course!" said Tony's father. "These old sheds and stables are right up their alley!"

Tony looked at his father in alarm. Did he know something about the little vampire's hiding place? But the grin on his father's face showed he had only been joking.

"There certainly isn't any such thing as vampires!" Tony declared.

His father looked surprised. "What about your friend?"

"What friend?"

"Your friend Rudolph Deathbed-Wagg."

"He is *not* my friend!" said Tony irritably. Why was everyone suddenly asking him about Rudolph Sackville-Bagg!

"Friend or not—haven't you always said he was a vampire?" asked Dad.

Luckily, at that very moment Mrs. Minnowpail came in with breakfast, so Tony was spared a reply. She set the platter on the table and said, "I'm sorry, but I can't offer you any eggs this morning. Someone has been in the henhouse and punctured all the eggs."

"Who would do a thing like that?" exclaimed Tony's father.

"I wish I knew," she replied with a questioning glance at Tony. "It was probably a kid's prank," she went on, "but not a very funny one, in my opinion!"

The emphasis on "kid" made Tony bristle.

"It could just as well have been a grown-up!" he retorted.

"Oh, yes?" said Mrs. Minnowpail. "Do you really believe a grown-up would come up with the idea of making little holes in all the eggs and sucking them dry?" She took a little brown egg out of her jacket pocket and held it out to Tony's father. "Here, take a look at this!"

"It's completely empty!" he said, shaking his head.

Tony did his best to look calm, but he was itching to examine the two holes in the egg more closely: they were about as big as the point of a pencil and about an inch apart.

"Could it have been a tramp?" suggested the smaller of the two ladies.

"Or a fox?" said the larger.

"A fox with two legs!" said Mrs. Minnowpail, eyeing Tony again. He felt himself color under her searching gaze. Now she was sure to think it had been him! But he always blushed when anyone stared hard at him!

"It wasn't me!" he cried hastily. "I was in bed by nine o'clock!"

Mrs. Minnowpail only smiled disbelievingly. "We'll probably never find out who it really was," she said. "But I only hope whoever it was is smart enough not to try it again, because next time he won't get away with it so easily!"

"What do you mean 'he'?" protested Tony. "It could just as well have been a girl!"

But the subject was closed as far as Mrs. Minnowpail was concerned. "I think you understand exactly what I mean," she said shortly. Then without another word she went back to the kitchen.

"That was a pretty stupid idea of yours," said Tony's father when she had gone.

"What was?" Tony didn't understand.

"That trick with the eggs."

"But it wasn't me!"

Tony's father said evenly, "I would like you to go to Mrs. Minnowpail now, and apologize."

"What?" Tony gasped. "Why should I apologize? I haven't done anything!" He jumped up. "You're not going to blame this one on me!" he cried, and ran out.

Back in his room he slammed the door and then threw himself on his bed. How mean can you get? he thought. He had protested his innocence loud and clear. But grown-ups only believed what they wanted to believe! Anyone could see that the two holes were the marks of a vampire's bite! It would be easy enough for Tony to show his parents who had made the holes in the eggs. He only had to take them to the old pigsty. . . .

No! He could never do that! When all was said and done, the little vampire had been his best friend—and maybe he still was. Tony realized that his anger at Rudolph Sackville-Bagg had almost evaporated. Now he was much more angry at his father and Mrs. Minnowpail for not believing him.

That night, he decided, he would find the little vampire and offer to make up. Once they were friends again he'd advise Rudolph to steer clear of the chicken coop in the future. The thought of Rudolph biting eggs made Tony laugh. Suddenly he felt like finishing the story about the bats.

19 / Something Must Be Done about Boredom

It was just before lunch and Tony was playing on the monkey bars when he saw his mother come out of the house. She came toward him with such determined strides that he quickly pulled himself up on top.

She came to a halt in front of him.

"Will you come down for a moment?" she said.

"Why?"

"I want a word with you."

"If I have to," he said, pretending to be cool. His father and Mrs. Minnowpail were bound to have told her about the eggs and now, as his mother, she was going to have a go at wringing a confession from him. But she was just going to be out of luck! With deliberate slowness Tony slid off the iron bar.

"What about?" he asked innocently.

"Dad's told me everything," she began.

That didn't surprise Tony in the least.

"So, we've been thinking . . . we were the ones who persuaded you to come on this trip . . ." Persuaded? Forced was more like it, thought Tony.

". . . and perhaps you really are too old for a vacation on a farm." She paused. "And so you're getting bored and that's why you keep coming up with these crazy ideas."

"What?" exclaimed Tony indignantly. "Just what crazy ideas are you talking about?"

"You know very well what I mean," she answered evasively.

"I do not!" he said vehemently, although of course he knew exactly what she was referring to. But for Pete's sake, he hadn't had anything to do with it! "If you think it was me who broke the eggs, you're just plain wrong."

But his mother only smiled. Apparently she had tactfully decided to leave the subject alone.

"And something must be done about boredom," she went on steadily. "That's why we've decided to take you on a moonlit stroll this evening."

She looked at him eagerly and seemed to expect him to be pleased. Normally he would have been—but not today!

"Couldn't we do it tomorrow?"

"No. Tomorrow Dad and I want to take you on a scavenger hunt."

Oh, no! groaned Tony softly. If only he could think up some excuse! "My—my leg hurts!"

"All of a sudden?"

"Yes, I twisted it."

"I see. But I'm sure your leg will be better by this evening. We won't set off till after supper."

"Couldn't we at least go before supper?"

"Why should we do that?"

"Well, it won't be so dark then." Even Tony realized how ridiculous that sounded, especially coming from him—he was the one who reveled in vampires, scary stories, and horror movies!

His mother merely gave him a mocking glance.

Then she turned around and went back to the house.

"Well, I can only go for half an hour!" Tony called after her. "At the very most!"

But naturally the moonlit stroll lasted much longer. They didn't get back to the farm until half past ten! Tony was totally worn out: they had lost their way three times and finally, in an attempt to jump over a little stream, he had fallen in the cold water. After all that both his legs were hurting!

He took off his soaking wet boots in the boiler room next to the kitchen. His overalls were also wet through up to the hips, so he hung them on a line.

"You look about as cheerful as a rained-out double-header!" teased his father.

"My throat hurts!" groaned Tony. He really did have a tickle in his throat.

"Have you caught a chill?" inquired his mother.

"For sure," he said in secret malicious glee. Let them worry about him! After all, this stupid night-time stroll had been their idea!

"Then you should have some warm milk and honey right away. I hope Mrs. Minnowpail is still awake."

"There's a light on in the living room," said Tony, giving a loud, painful-sounding cough.

His mother jumped. "You go straight to bed."

"What about my milk?"

"I'll bring it to you."

Tony grinned contentedly. He liked warm milk and honey, especially in bed! But he had to wait an unusually long time for it. He had almost fallen asleep when his mother finally brought in a large glass of milk. Cautiously he took a sip.

"But this is cold!" he exclaimed indignantly.

"Oh? Is it?"

"Yes. Usually you make it so hot I can't drink it."

"Then it must have cooled down," said his mother. "Mrs. Minnowpail had so much to tell me, you see."

Tony pricked up his ears. "What about?"

"Someone's been in the henhouse again and sucked all the eggs dry."

Tony jumped. "Did Mrs. Minnowpail see him?"

"Who?"

"The . . ." *Little vampire* was on the tip of Tony's tongue. "The . . . thief."

"No. When Mrs. Minnowpail went to the henhouse at about ten o'clock, it had already happened. And all the eggs have the same little holes as yesterday."

"So now you can't suspect me anymore!"

"No, it can't have been you," said his mother with a smile—rather an embarrassed one, Tony was pleased to notice. "But we'll soon find out who's been wreaking havoc in the henhouse!" she declared.

"How?"

"Mrs. Minnowpail has told a neighbor. He's coming tomorrow and bringing his dog with him."

"Oh, no!" Tony couldn't stop himself. Poor Rudolph!

"Why does that bother you?" asked his mother. "Are you scared of dogs suddenly?"

"Not of dogs," said Tony. "But I am of neighbors!"

20 / The Butterfly Collector

Tony found out just how right he was the next afternoon when he bumped into Joanna in the yard.

"Who is this neighbor of yours who's coming this evening?" he asked.

"Oh, him," said Joanna lightly. "He's our old village doctor."

Tony gave a sigh of relief—but only for a moment, because she went on, "Actually he's got the same hobby as you!"

"What's that?" he asked suspiciously.

She giggled. "Vampires!"

Tony gave a start.

"He's called Dr. Rummage," she continued easily. "Dr. Ernest Albert Rummage. The name's just right for him because he's always rummaging around." She laughed, but Tony was not in the mood for a joke.

"What do you mean about vampires?" he asked.

"You ought to take a look in his house!" said Joanna. "He has all the books there are about vampires and bats. And in his living room there's a display case—and I bet you can't guess what's inside it!"

"I dunno," said Tony, who already suspected that whatever Dr. Rummage kept in his display case, it was nothing very nice.

Joanna explained in a whisper, "Impaled moths!"

"Impaled moths?" repeated Tony, shocked.

"Yes. Just imagine, he sticks a pointed matchstick through their bodies!"

Tony gulped. "Er—what kind of moths?"

"You know—just butterflies."

"I see," said Tony in relief. For a moment he had been afraid they might be impaled baby vampires! Even so, Dr. Rummage was sounding more and more unpleasant. And the situation was becoming very grave for Rudolph Sackville-Bagg! "Do you know when he's supposed to come?"

"After supper," said Joanna.

"Great," said Tony, wondering how he was going to prevent Dr. Rummage from adding Rudolph to his display case.

21 / Dr. Rummage

There was spaghetti for dinner, but Tony hardly managed to eat a mouthful. He fidgeted in his chair and kept looking outside. When a car pulled up, his heart was in his mouth. But it was only Mr. Minnowpail.

"I think you must have a temperature," remarked Tony's mother, who had been watching him.

"Oh, no, I don't think so," he was quick to reassure her. On no account must she think he was sick, or she would send him straight to bed!

"It's better," he lied.

"Is it?" she asked doubtfully. "Your eyes look very bright and feverish."

"I feel terrific!" he assured her.

Maybe she was right after all. Maybe he was sick. But at the moment it didn't matter. Only one thing was important now: He had to warn the little vampire before Dr. Rummage and his dog appeared!

"May I go outside?" he asked, trying not to let his parents see how nervous he was.

"Aren't you still hungry?" asked his mother.

"I'll—I'll take an apple with me!" replied Tony quickly. He could always be sure of getting on the right side of his parents with fruit and vegetables! It seemed to work this time too, for his mother said gently, "Well, all right. But when it starts to get dark, come straight back inside."

"Okay," he promised, thinking to himself that in any case, once it was really dark out, he wouldn't be able to achieve anything, because by then the vampire would have flown off into the night. No, Tony would have to catch him while he was still in his coffin.

As he went out of the front door, a small black van was just turning into the drive. It looks like a hearse! thought Tony, freezing in his tracks. It could only be Dr. Rummage! He was of medium height and had gray hair combed back from his forehead. His prominent black eyebrows and long hooked nose gave his face a dark, menacing expression, or so Tony thought, and he couldn't help taking a step or two backward. But Dr. Rummage paid no attention to him. He went to the back of his van and opened it. An enormous black dog jumped out.

Tony stood as if rooted to the spot, and stared at the dog. It was the size of a Great Dane, but its coat was long and shaggy. All you could see of its face were its teeth, and they were so large and pointy that they gave Tony goose bumps.

The dog must have been well trained, because when its master said, "Heel!" it followed him to the door without a leash. As he went past, Dr. Rummage glanced at Tony, nodded curtly at him, and then disappeared into the house. After the door had closed behind the man and his dog, Tony took a deep breath. That wasn't a dog—it was a monster!

Luckily the monster was safe inside now. And Dr. Rummage was sure to spend a couple of minutes chatting with Mrs. Minnowpail. . . . And that was all the time Tony had to convince the little vampire that he mustn't remain on the farm a single moment longer!

I just hope Rudolph is already awake, thought Tony as he raced around the barn to the old pigsty.

22 / A Visit from a Lady

Tony cautiously pushed up the rusty old catch which held the pigsty closed. It was a catch that could be opened from the outside or the inside. Slowly, and with a squeak, the door opened. . . . The strong smell of decay that hit him told Tony that the little vampire was still at home. And he must be awake, for a feeble light came from the corner where his coffin was hidden.

Tony shut the door behind him and called, "Rudolph! It's me, Tony!"

The only answer was a high-pitched giggle.

Tony hesitated. That didn't sound like the little vampire!

"Rudolph!" he called again. "It's me!"

"Come on in!" said a croaky voice—the voice of the little vampire.

"Are you alone?" asked Tony nervously.

Again he heard the high-pitched giggle. Then the little vampire said, "There's a lady waiting for you."

"A lady?" repeated Tony, startled. "Not—Aunt Dorothy?"

"Come see for yourself!" answered the little vampire with a grating laugh. The fact that Rudolph was laughing reassured Tony. It certainly couldn't be Aunt Dorothy!

"Is it Anna?" he asked in a husky voice.

A fresh bout of giggles was the reply. So it was Anna! Tony let out his breath, and with beating heart, went into the stall.

Anna was sitting at the foot of the coffin. Her little round face seemed to glow in the candlelight. She looked at him so adoringly with her huge eyes that he went quite hot.

"Good evening, Tony!" she said with a smile.

"Hi, Anna!" he replied, turning red.

"I just had to see you," she said, turning red too.

"M-me?" Tony couldn't think of a better reply.

"You didn't think she was missing *me*?" croaked Rudolph from the coffin.

"I brought something with me," said Anna, and took a red book from under her cape. "My autograph book." She showed it to him proudly. "You can be the first human to write in it!"

"There's already a poem by me in it!" announced Rudolph. "Do you want to hear it?" And without waiting for an answer he recited in a smug voice:

> *"If you give me blood*
> *I feel very good.*
> *But wine on the chill*
> *Makes me feel quite ill."*

Anna looked at him sideways and said bitingly, "If I were you, I wouldn't call attention to that one!"

"And why not?" asked the little vampire with a glitter in his eyes.

"Because it isn't a real poem. *Blood* and *good* don't rhyme."

"So what?" growled the vampire. "*Chill* and *ill* do!"

"In a real poem all the lines have to rhyme," Anna contradicted him.

The vampire shrugged his shoulders. "Then I'll simply recite it like this," he said, making *blood* rhyme with *good*:

> *"If you give me blood*
> *I feel very good.*
> *But wine on the chill*
> *Makes me feel quite ill."*

"Yuck!" said Anna contemptuously. "That's not even English!" The little vampire looked hurt. He shut his mouth and fell silent.

"Will you write something for me in here?" Anna said to Tony, looking at him entreatingly.

But Tony did not reply. He had suddenly gone deathly white.

"What's up?" she asked.

"There's someone outside!" he said in a shaky voice.

The little vampire gave a cry of alarm. "Outside the pigsty?"

"Yes. And I know who it is: Dr. Rummage! He's come here tonight to find out who keeps sucking the eggs dry in the henhouse."

"Why didn't you tell us this before?" hissed the vampire.

"Because—" Tony began, then stopped. Should he admit that Anna had completely confused him? That when she looked at him with those big eyes, he forgot everything else?

But Rudolph didn't want to wait for an answer. He leapt out of his coffin and called to his sister, "We have to fly!"

"But you won't get very far!" Tony warned him gloomily. "Dr. Rummage has got a dog, a real monster, as big as a horse."

"Then we'll have to barricade the door!" cried the vampire, tugging at the large chest which lay beside his coffin. "Give me some help!"

Anna did not move. Gently she said, "I've got a much better idea—if Tony will go along with it," she added with a fervent look at Tony.

"What sort of idea?" asked Tony suspiciously.

"You must go outside and have a talk with this Dr. Rummage."

88

"Me?" cried Tony. "But I—" *I'm scared of him too!* was what he wanted to say, but then he stopped himself because he didn't want to look stupid. Instead he asked cautiously, "What should I talk to him about?"

"It doesn't matter. Just get him away from here."

Tony hesitated. It wasn't a bad idea—and it was probably the only chance the vampires had of getting away. Even so . . . "It's always me who has to do everything," he grumbled.

Anna smiled sweetly at him. "That's because you're a human! And you humans have such an easier time of it than we do in almost everything!"

"You can say that again," agreed Rudolph.

Tony sighed, resigned to his fate. "Okay," he said, "I'll go."

23 / The Man in the Black Coat

Tony had hardly closed the pigsty door behind him
when something black came bounding toward him;
at a command from behind, it sat panting just a step
away from him. It was Dr. Rummage's dog! Tony
didn't dare to move. He had the feeling that the
monster would tear him to bits if he so much as
twitched his little finger! He was quite relieved when
Dr. Rummage appeared.

"What are you doing here?" asked Dr. Rummage.

"I—I was looking around for something," murmured Tony.

"What?"

"A—er—a piece of paper with someone's phone
number."

"And you lost it right here?"

"Well, somewhere around here—"

"You've already looked in that shed?" Dr. Rummage pointed to the old pigsty. "I did hear you searching in there."

Tony tried to keep calm. "That's right," he said,
"but the piece of paper wasn't there."

"Did anything in the shed strike you as suspicious?"

"Suspicious? No, not at all," Tony assured him.

Dr. Rummage glanced irresolutely over at the
pigsty. "I was just about to investigate what was going

on in that shed," he declared. "But if you're positive you didn't see anything suspicious. . . . There's a lot of old junk in there, isn't there?"

"Yes. Just a lot of junk."

"Then I can save myself the trouble."

"You certainly can!" Tony agreed, trying to keep back a smile.

"Tell me something, do you have any idea who keeps sucking the eggs dry?" Dr. Rummage's voice took on a confidential tone, almost friendly. Tony had obviously managed to convince him.

"I think I just might," Tony said.

"Really? Who?"

"The man in the black coat."

Dr. Rummage pricked up his ears. "The man in the black coat? What sort of coat? Was it very long and full?"

Tony could see what he was getting at, and gleefully led the doctor on.

"Yes, it went all the way to the floor. It wasn't exactly a coat, it was more like a cape."

"Really?" Dr. Rummage whistled softly through his teeth. "And what did this man look like?"

"He was very pale and had long straggly hair."

"Did he smell all musty?" By now Dr. Rummage was really excited.

"I almost had to hold my nose," Tony replied.

"Did you, now?" said Dr. Rummage. "Where did you see this man?"

"In the barn. I happened to be looking when he disappeared into the hay."

It was all Tony could do not to laugh. Dr. Rummage seemed to believe every word of it!

"What time of day did you see him?"

"Just after sundown." That of course was the only possible answer if he wanted Dr. Rummage to believe he had seen a vampire.

"Could you show me the place where he disappeared?" asked Dr. Rummage with barely contained excitement.

"Of course."

As Tony moved away, he gave one look back at the old pigsty.

What would they do without me? he thought.

24 / Vampire Verses

Of course Dr. Rummage did not find anyone in the barn. His dog merely stumbled on a couple of cats who crouched in a box and hissed.

Now Tony was in bed. He was just thinking back with delight over the events of the day when someone tapped softly on his window. He ran over and drew the curtain. Outside sat Anna!

Startled, Tony opened the window. "You can't stay here!" he cried. "Mom's coming any minute!"

"I only wanted to bring you my autograph book," she replied with a smile, handing him the red book. "Will you write in it?"

"Yes," he told her, feeling embarrassed—and then there was a knock on his door.

Immediately he heard his mother's horrified voice. "Tony! Do you want to catch bronchitis?"

"I—er—I was so hot," stuttered Tony, stuffing the autograph book down his pajama pants.

"You're feeling hot because you've got a temperature!" scolded his mother, shutting the window so quickly that she didn't notice the small shadow shrinking back from the windowsill. "Have you taken your temperature?"

"Yes," Tony nodded, and went slowly back to his bed. I just hope the book doesn't fall out of my pajamas! he thought.

Luckily his mother was busy with the thermometer. "A hundred degrees!" she exclaimed.

By now Tony had reached the bed and let himself sink down into the soft mattress in relief. "Is that high?" he asked innocently.

"You'll have to stay in bed tomorrow," she told him. "And now, put your light out and go to sleep."

"Yes, Mom," he said, and switched off the light.

"Not while I'm still in the room!" said his mother crossly, as she felt her way through the darkness to the door.

"Then may I put it on again?" he asked with a grin. But she snapped the door shut behind her without saying another word.

Tony waited till she had gone downstairs. Then he turned on the light and took out the autograph book. It had a red velvet cover which was already torn in a few places. A musty smell came from the material which reminded him of Anna. Was she still crouching on the windowsill?

He went to the window and peered outside, but there was no one to be seen. He went back to bed again and turned the first page in great anticipation.

THIS AUTOGRAPH BOOK BELONGS TO ANNA EMILY SACKVILLE-BAGG, it said in a child's round handwriting, and underneath:

> If a poem you do complete,
> Please be sure to keep it neat.

This request had obviously not been much help, for already the second page was covered in ink blots.

Life is at its best for me,
When blood doth flow in quantity.
Written to remind you of your brother,
Gregory.

Tony flicked over a few more pages.

If in life you wish to find
True happiness of heart and mind,
Then drink the blood of mortal man
To give you joy, as well it can.
From your Aunt Dorothy.

Tony felt himself shudder pleasantly. It was a thrill to read these bloodthirsty verses, safe in the knowledge that the vampires who had written them were flying about outside and couldn't touch him. He read on avidly.

If e'er you hear the sound of song
Look there for blood, you won't be wrong!
This advice comes to you from your
grandmother, Sabina the Sinister.

There then followed Rudolph's poem which Tony knew already, with the signature: *A souvenir from your brother, Rudolph the Rotten*. Tony had never before heard this nickname of Rudolph's, and he supposed that Rudolph had used it just to make himself sound important. Nearly all the vampires seemed to have a nickname: for example, William the Wild, whose verse stood on the following page:

> *Come rain or come sunshine,*
> *Fire, wind, hail, or flood,*
> *Take care that on your lips*
> *There's always fresh blood!*
> Words of wisdom from your grandfather.

The following page boasted a large spot of blood. Underneath was written:

> *White swan swimming on bluest lake:*
> *Dearest Anna, for my sake,*
> *Keep your blood as fresh and pure*
> *As swan's plumage, evermore.*
> So writes your Uncle Theodore.

Uncle Theodore! He was the vampire who had sat playing cards on his tombstone and been caught in the act by McRookery the night watchman! Since that day his coffin in the Sackville-Bagg family vault had lain empty. . . . That made the spot of blood even more grisly, thought Tony.

Quickly he turned the page.

> *Conversing is silver:*
> *But bleeding is gold.*
> So writes your father, Frederick the Frightful.

Back home in my autograph book there are only the most boring, stupid rhymes, Tony thought enviously. There aren't any that would give you the creeps! Not like the one written in an ancient, twirly handwriting by Thelma the Thirsty:

Keep your teeth polished and keep your teeth nice.
'Twill make you both healthy and wealthy
and wise.
To remind you of your mother.

The rest of the pages were empty—except for one little word, *Tony*, which Anna had written at the top of the next page. If only he knew what to write! But the only rhymes he could think of were as boring as the ones in his own autograph book.

"Roses are red, violets are blue, tulips are yellow," he murmured out loud, and tried desperately to think of something to rhyme.

"Primroses too?" That wasn't very interesting.

"What color are you?" Not much better!

"How do you do?" No, that didn't work.

Tony sighed. It was going to be hard work, thinking up a suitable verse! He took a notepad and pencil out of his bedside-table drawer.

A little house of roses, a little door of daisies . . . he wrote, and then quickly crossed it out.

> *Be like a little violet*
> *Modest, good always,*
> *And not like other vampires,*
> *Always wanting praise. . . .*

That sounded a bit better, but the vampires might be insulted by it. Anything but that!

Always be dutiful, always be wise,
Following always your parents' advice,
Learn when to keep silent, when to speak out,
There's a time and a place, of that
there's no doubt.

Tony's eyes began to close. For him the time and the place had come to go to sleep—once he had hidden Anna's autograph book in his suitcase.

25 / Dr. Rummage's Discovery

When Tony woke up the next morning, there was a breakfast tray by his bed. Did his mother really think he was too sick to get up for breakfast? His throat still hurt, it was true, as he took his first sip of cocoa, but he was sure to feel better as soon as he got up. He certainly didn't want to stay in bed! What was more, he had to find out if there were any more surprises in store for tonight.

He got dressed and went downstairs. His parents were at the breakfast table, and they looked up in dismay as he came in. The two other ladies must have already eaten, for their places had been cleared away.

"You should stay in bed!" said Tony's mother reproachfully.

"But I'm not sick."

"Have you taken your temperature?" asked his father.

"Yes," he lied.

"And what was it?"

"Ninety-eight point six."

His parents exchanged looks. "I don't believe it!" declared his mother. "You look pale, and your eyes are too bright, just like yesterday."

"I'm not sick!" said Tony furiously.

"Well, if you say so . . ." His mother sounded hurt. "Would you like a roll?"

I—I'm not hungry, was what Tony nearly said, but of course he couldn't admit that. "Thank you."

His father spread a roll with jam and gave it to him.

"Anyway—did Dr. Rummage find the thief?" inquired Tony cautiously.

His mother looked at him significantly. "No. But he did find something else—something that will be of great interest to you, I would think!" she added pointedly.

Tony became even more pale. "What?"

She pointed to an old, dog-eared book lying on the windowseat.

"That's yours, isn't it?"

It was *Voices from the Vault*, which he had lent the little vampire a few weeks earlier!

"Where did you get that from?"

"It was in the henhouse. Dr. Rummage found it behind a couple of boxes."

"But . . ." said Tony, and then stopped. There was no point in explaining to them that he had lent the book to someone, because then they would immediately ask, to whom!

"So we were right!" said his father.

"Yes. The book belongs to me."

"Then we were right too that you have been in the henhouse?"

If they only knew! He wouldn't set foot in the chicken coop again for all the tea in China! But of course, he couldn't say that! So he lied. "Yes."

"Ah-ha!" said his father, obviously satisfied. "And

while you were there, you . . . er . . . you played around a bit with the eggs."

"What?" retorted Tony angrily. "I'm still supposed to have messed around with the eggs, am I? I never touched them!"

"Oh, really?" his father countered coolly. "Then who did?"

Tony was so livid at his father's stubborn suspiciousness that he forgot to be cautious. "If you must know, it was the little vampire!" And with that he ran out the door.

At first he wanted to go to his room, but then he realized his parents would certainly follow him there in order to talk to him. And he hadn't the slightest desire to be cross-examined any further! Then he remembered that in the barn there were two old bicycles which guests were allowed to use. Yes, that's what he'd do: just ride off—and his parents, who always wanted to know where he was going, would have a real fright! Perhaps then they'll realize how mean and unfair it is to suspect me! he thought as he rode off toward Oniontown on a green bicycle with no bell or brakes. But he didn't get far. After only a short way he felt so dizzy that he had to get off. He stood by the bicycle uncertainly. Should he keep going on foot?

But then he decided he didn't feel like running away anymore. Suddenly he was so tired. . . . So he brought the bike back to the barn and went to his room.

26 / A House Call

"He's got a temperature of one hundred point nine degrees!" he heard his mother saying.

"Then we have to call a doctor!" That was his father's voice.

Tony blinked. He saw his parents standing by the bed. They looked down at him with some concern.

"Am I sick?" he asked.

"Yes. We're going to call the doctor."

"No, I don't want a doctor!" screamed Tony. His parents obviously didn't know how Tony felt about the village doctor!

"Why ever not?"

"Because . . . I'm feeling much better!"

"So suddenly?" said his mother in disbelief. "No, I think the doctor had better take a look at you."

"You've never been frightened of doctors before," remarked his father with some amazement.

"It's never been . . ." said Tony. "Well, never been some idiot village doctor before!"

"Tony!" cried his mother. "Whatever has gotten into you?"

"It's true, though!" he said. "In this village I bet they can't tell the difference between a stethoscope and a pitchfork!"

"I think you're hallucinating!" said his father irritably.

"I only hope so!" growled Tony.

But unfortunately it was no figment of his imagination when Dr. Rummage came and stood by his bed shortly afterward. No, he was all too real with his broad face and piercing blue eyes.

"So you're ill, are you?" he asked in a clumsily friendly voice.

"I dunno" was all Tony would say.

"You don't know?" Dr. Rummage seemed to think it was funny.

Tony had already decided to be as unhelpful as possible. "I dunno what Mom's been telling you!"

"Tony, please!" protested his mother.

"Well, open your mouth," said Dr. Rummage, looking in his little black bag.

Reluctantly Tony did as he was told.

"His throat is inflamed," announced Dr. Rummage when he had peered into Tony's mouth. "You really must have caught a cold last night." Tony blushed.

"Did you find that piece of paper, by the way?" Dr. Rummage went on. It didn't seem to bother him that Tony couldn't answer with a tongue depressor in his mouth. "Little boys shouldn't wander about alone in the dark," he remarked, as he sprayed a stinging liquid down Tony's throat. "Who knows who might be out and about? Although in fact I never caught a glimpse of the man you were telling me about."

"What man?" asked Tony's father, suddenly alert. Tony wanted to sink through the floor! He'd been waiting for this question!

"Don't you know?" said Dr. Rummage in surprise. "There was supposed to be some man hiding in the barn. He was very pale, with long straggly hair and a black cape."

"Did Tony tell you that?" asked his mother.

"Yes."

"He just made it up!" she exclaimed. "He must have read about it in one of his crazy books!"

All eyes turned on Tony.

"Is that true?" asked his father. "Did you make it up?"

"Yes," admitted Tony after a slight hesitation.

"But why?" asked Dr. Rummage.

"To make himself seem important!" replied his father.

Tony bit his lips. It was a mean suggestion—and yet he couldn't defend himself without giving the little vampire away.

"I wanted to play a trick on you," he said through clenched teeth.

"Nice trick!" remarked Dr. Rummage grimly. "Especially if the real thief got away because of it!"

Tony had to smile. If only Dr. Rummage knew how right he was!

"I thought you knew all along who's been stealing the eggs," he said innocently.

"What do you mean?"

"Well . . . my father knows who the culprit is, don't you, Dad?"

"What are you talking about?" exclaimed his father angrily.

"Isn't it true that you suspect someone?"

"And who might that be?" His father had even turned a little pink, Tony noticed with secret satisfaction.

"Yes, who?" asked Dr. Rummage excitedly.

Tony smiled. "Me," he said smoothly.

"That's ridiculous!" exclaimed his father turning to Dr. Rummage. "I only wanted to know what his book was doing in the henhouse!"

"Please don't fight!" pleaded Mom. "After all, Tony isn't well."

"Exactly!" said Tony. "And now I need some rest!" With that he lay back on his pillows and shut his eyes—although not so tightly that he couldn't see Dr. Rummage snap his bag shut.

"I'll drop by again in the morning," he said.

When he had gone, Tony's mother said, "Now you won't be able to have fun with us this evening."

"I didn't really want to anyway," grunted Tony.

"Even so, it's a shame. Just like you to go and get sick while we're on vacation!"

"It isn't my fault!" muttered Tony, and he turned to face the wall.

27 / Get Well Soon!

At half past eight, as the smell of sausages being grilled in the garden reached Tony's room, someone knocked softly on the door.

"Yes?" he said.

Joanna came in with a paper plate and a cup in her hand. "I thought you might be hungry," she said, and put the things down on his bedside table. As she did so, her glance fell on Anna's autograph book, which was also lying there.

"Is that about vampires?" she asked curiously.

"No," said Tony hastily, stuffing the book under his pillow. "It's an autograph book."

"An autograph book?" Joanna giggled. "Only girls write in autograph books around here!"

"Boys are more open minded in the city!"

"May I look at it?"

"No."

"Oh, please!"

"All I can do is read you a couple of rhymes," said Tony with a wicked grin.

"Oh, yes!"

Tony took out the book and held it so that she wouldn't be able to see the pages. "Life is at its best for me,/When blood doth flow in quantity!"

Joanna's eyes were wide open. "Does it really say that?"

"Do you want to hear another?" he asked with a slight laugh, and without waiting for her answer, he read, "Come rain or come sunshine,/Fire, wind, hail, or flood,/Take care that on your lips /There's always fresh blood!"

"Eeeugh! What gross rhymes!" cried Joanna. "I wouldn't want them in my autograph book!"

Tony grinned. "Some people like them!"

"Well, whose book is it?"

"It—it belongs to my girlfriend."

"Your girlfriend?" asked Joanna in astonishment. "I didn't know you had a—"

"You can't know everything," he said.

"Do I know her?"

"Of course not."

"What's her name?"

"Anna."

"Oh, well," she said in embarrassment, going to the door. "Get well soon!"

"Thanks for the food!" Tony called after her.

28 / Tulips and Roses Bloom in Spring

Joanna had hardly closed the door behind her when someone knocked on the window. Tony waited till her footsteps had died away. Then he got up and went quietly over to the window. He pulled the curtain to one side and peered out.

At first all he could see was the dark night sky and the moon. But then he saw something else—Anna's face! She was sitting on the windowsill and had drawn her cape tightly around her, as if she were freezing cold.

Tony opened the window.

"May I come in?" she asked.

"If you like," he said, irritated that his voice sounded so hoarse.

"Of course I like!" She smiled and sprang lightly into the room. She looked around and said, "You had a visitor!"

"How do you know?"

"I heard you."

Tony felt himself go red. "Did you hear what we were talking about?"

"Yes. You told her I was your girlfriend!"

"I only said that because she wanted to know who the autograph book belonged to!" he said, trying to make an excuse. He found it extremely painful that she had heard it all!

But Anna didn't seem to find anything wrong. "It doesn't matter if she knows about us," she said casually, as if it were the most natural thing in the world. Then she went over to the bed where the autograph book lay. "Have you written in it?"

"No. I can't think of anything."

"But there are so many rhymes! Shall I tell you one?

"Tulips and roses bloom in spring!
Mother may know everything.
Just one secret keep from view—
When a boy first kisses you!"

She broke into fits of giggles, but Tony merely raised an eyebrow.

"I'm not writing anything like that!" he declared.

"Why aren't you down in the garden, anyway?" she asked suddenly. "There's a party going on."

"Don't feel like it," grunted Tony, who didn't want her to find out about his sore throat and start feeling sorry for him.

"But it looks like a great party!" she enthused. "There's a huge bonfire, and lanterns hanging in the trees."

"It's just for little kids!" he said disparagingly.

"No. There are grown-ups there too! I'd like to go and join in."

"Why don't you, then?"

"I'm not that stupid!" she retorted. "Besides, there isn't time. I've got to help Rudolph take his coffin back to the vault."

"You're taking his coffin back to the vault?" exclaimed Tony in dismay. "But why?"

"Because of Dr. Rummage. Rudolph hasn't slept a wink all day, and he can't wait to go home."

"Why didn't he tell me all this himself?"

"Because he's scared silly. He thinks Dr. Rummage is sitting out there in the garden!"

"But he'll never find his way back without me!"

"Is that so?" said Anna haughtily. "Well, he's got me and I'm very good at finding my way in the dark! I did manage to get here, after all!"

"But you don't know the dangers of the countryside! There are lots of people around here who really do believe in vampires!"

Anna looked at him tenderly. "Are you worried about me?"

"I . . . just don't want anything to happen to you, that's all," he stuttered.

Anna's large eyes glittered. "Ah, Tony," she sighed, and quickly turned her head away. "No one's ever been worried about me before," she said quietly.

Tony coughed in embarrassment. "I could take you to the station," he said, to turn the conversation to a less tricky subject. "From there you can fly along the railroad tracks."

"It really isn't necessary!" she protested.

"Even so," said Tony, "three people can do more than two!"

"All right, then!" she said, and looking steadily at him, she added, "And at least the two of us will be together for a little longer!"

"We—we ought to get going!" he murmured.

"In your pajamas?" she said with a laugh.

Tony looked down with a start. For the first time he noticed he was wearing his pajamas in front of Anna—his awful crumpled old baggy pajamas!

Anna seemed to sense his embarrassment. She climbed up to the window and said, "We'll wait for you at the pigsty." And then she was gone.

29 / News from the Vault

Tony put on his thickest sweater and tied a scarf around his neck. His sore throat felt worse than ever despite the pills Dr. Rummage had given him. They were probably the wrong kind! he thought spitefully, pills for an upset stomach or hoof-and-mouth disease! Even so, he popped another in his mouth before he went downstairs.

He stopped at the front door and listened. Luckily the garden was on the other side of the house. He could hear the sound of music wafting over, and also a woman laughing. He hoped the party would go on for quite a while—at least until he was back from the station! And if it didn't? Well, he'd think up some excuse.

Anna and Rudolph were waiting for him at the door of the pigsty, in the shadow of which they had laid the coffin.

"Here you are at last!" growled Rudolph.

"Don't be so mean to Tony!" Anna scolded him. "After all, he's trying to help you."

"Sure, sure. First he talks me into coming with him to this ridiculous farm, and now I'm supposed to be grateful!"

"I talked you into coming, did I?" cried Tony angrily. "And who had to get away from George the Boisterous?"

The vampire gave a broad grin. "Nobody. In fact, George the Boisterous has left the vault!"

Tony gasped in indignation at the way the little vampire kept twisting the facts. "That's not true!"

"Isn't it?" smiled the vampire. "Ask Anna whether he's left or not!"

"I don't mean that!" Tony yelled furiously. Of course Rudolph knew exactly what Tony was talking about, but it was pointless quarreling with him now.

"He really has left," said Anna, who didn't know what all the fuss was about.

"You see!" exulted the vampire. "So now you can help Anna carry the coffin."

"And what will you do?" asked Anna.

"I'll show you the way."

"That would just suit you, wouldn't it? Either you carry the front end, or I won't carry it at all!"

"What about Tony?" protested the vampire.

"Tony will show us the way!" she declared, and went to the back of the coffin. "Well? Is the coffin going to stay here?"

"I'm coming," grumbled the vampire grudgingly, and picked up the front end.

"We're ready!" Anna smiled at Tony, who had just checked once more that no one was about.

"Good!" he said. "The coast is clear!"

30 / Low Blood Pressure

They went around the barn and across the yard, where Tony's parents' car and the Minnowpails' van were parked. Once through the tall trees beyond, and they had reached the road to the village. After they had been walking for a while, the little vampire put down his end of the coffin.

"My back aches!" he groaned.

"You only want Tony to carry the coffin for you!" scolded Anna.

"But I haven't slept all day," he complained, "and I haven't eaten either! I'm getting black spots in front of my eyes!"

"Tell me another one" was all she said.

"I've got low blood pressure!" cried the little vampire. "So I might easily faint!"

"Really?" asked Anna disbelievingly. "And how are you supposed to know you have low blood pressure?"

"I can feel it."

"And I can feel you're just a lazy beast!" she retorted crossly.

The vampire made a hurt face. "That's not for you to say. After all, you're still half a baby."

"That's what you think, Grandpa!" Anna yelled and slammed the coffin into Rudolph from behind.

"Have you two gone crazy?" hissed Tony. "You're

making enough noise to wake the whole neigh-
borhood!"

That got through to Rudolph and Anna. Suddenly
they were still as mice.

"Has anybody heard us?" asked the little vampire
worriedly.

Tony nodded in the direction of a house which lay
hidden behind a hedge; all that could be seen of it
was a lighted attic window. "I wouldn't be surprised."

"We must go on," urged Anna.

"No, wait," said the vampire. "Maybe I could find
a snack in there first. . . ."

"I wouldn't," advised Anna.

"I would!" retorted the vampire. "And then I'll be
in much better shape to carry the coffin."

With half-open lips and a staring, vacant look in
his eyes, he crept slowly up to the house. Anna hastily
pulled the coffin behind a bush.

"Come on, we'd better follow him," she whispered
to Tony. "Otherwise there'll be another disaster!"

31 / Spies

The little vampire moved like a sleepwalker up the carefully raked path to the house, followed by Tony and Anna. It was a modern, red-brick house with a front door made of metal and glass, over which a small light glowed. The ground-floor windows were dark. Only one attic window showed a light burning.

Rudolph did not stop to investigate the front of the house. He went straight around to the back.

"He says nobody ever remembers to lock the back door," Tony said softly to Anna.

She looked at him in astonishment. "Is that true?"

"No. But he'll find out soon enough for himself."

"Shouldn't we follow him?"

"I'd rather stay behind these bushes," answered Tony. "Anyway, he's bound to come straight back."

After a moment Anna remarked, "I'd just love to have a look inside. I'm very interested in interior decoration."

"You mean you want to go in?"

"No, just peek through the windows," she said. "Will you wait for me?"

Tony nodded. She quickly ran over to the house and peered in through the windows. She came back looking disappointed.

"Ehh, it's very boring," she said. "In the dining room there's just a table and four chairs. In the next room there's a desk near the door and nothing else but bookshelves."

Tony yawned, just to show he wasn't the least bit interested.

"And then there's the living room," she went on. "With a sofa, a table, and two armchairs. Oh, yes, and a big display case against the wall." Tony was only half listening but he gave a start when she said, "A big display case full of butterflies!"

"Butterflies?" he stammered.

"Yes. I could see them clearly, because the moon was shining into the room. And just imagine—someone has pinned them up with matchsticks!"

"Oh, no!" Tony groaned. "It's Dr. Rummage's house!" Anna's eyes widened in fright.

"Dr. Rummage's house? And Rudolph . . ."

"Let's just hope the door is locked," said Tony gloomily.

Just then they heard a furious barking coming from the back of the house. Tony jumped. "Dr. Rummage's dog! The black monster!"

"I'll go and see if anything's happened to Rudolph!" declared Anna, turning to go.

"Wait!" called Tony, grabbing her cloak firmly.

Impatiently she asked, "Well, have you got a better idea?"

"We mustn't do anything stupid!" he said imploringly. "Or do you want Dr. Rummage to get his hands on you too?"

"Do you think . . . ?" She left the sentence unfinished, for at that moment a light went on in the consulting room. And what they saw inside took their breath away. Dr. Rummage came into the room— pushing the little vampire in front of him!

Rudolph's head was bowed, like that of an animal being led to the slaughter.

"Oh, how terrible!" whispered Anna. "What's he going to do to him?"

As if he had heard her words, Dr. Rummage pulled the curtains shut with a jerk.

"First, he'll sound him out," suggested Tony.

"Yes, but then what?"

Tony said no more, the thought was too dreadful. He had seen only too clearly the sharpened wooden stakes protruding from Dr. Rummage's jacket pocket.

"I'd like to smash the window!" said Anna, shaking her tiny fists.

"That wouldn't be any use," answered Tony. "We'll have to do something else, something crafty. And I think I know what. . . ."

"What?" breathed Anna, her eyes wide open.

"I'll go and ring the bell. Then Dr. Rummage will come to the door . . ."

". . . and Rudolph can escape!" she finished excitedly. "Oh, Tony, I'm scared!"

So am I, thought Tony, but he decided it was better not to say so. He stuck out his chin in determination and marched confidently up to the front door. He felt like a bullfighter on his way to the arena.

"Good luck!" Anna called after him.

"Thanks!" he said softly, and pressed the doorbell.

32 / Doctor's Hours

Tony heard the bell ring inside the house. To his ears it sounded harsh and shrill, and his heart began to pound. But nothing moved. He gulped. Then he rang a second time. Footsteps came toward him. Tony wanted to turn and run, but he thought of the little vampire and gritted his teeth.

Dr. Rummage opened the door, but only an inch. He looked at Tony distrustfully through narrowed eyes. "What do you want?" he asked gruffly.

"I . . ." Tony had thought out beforehand exactly what to say, but under Dr. Rummage's piercing gaze he still ended up stuttering. "I . . . it's about my—my sore throat!"

Dr. Rummage's forbidding expression lightened. "Oh, of course! Yes, now I recognize you. You're the boy on vacation who's got a bad throat." He opened the door a little wider. "But tell me, what are you doing out here? Why aren't you in bed?"

"My—my mother sent me," lied Tony. "I'm—I'm supposed to fetch some different pills. The ones you gave me aren't helping."

"Of course they aren't helping if you're up and about all the time!" said Dr. Rummage crossly. "But I will give you some more, nonetheless. Wait here!"

"J-just a minute!" called Tony. He noticed he was breaking out in a sweat. At all costs he must keep

Dr. Rummage at the door as long as possible if the little vampire was going to manage to escape. "My— my mother also said you should take another look at my sore throat!"

"And that's why she sent you over here in the cold night air?" Dr. Rummage shook his head. "What stupidity! If I didn't have a visitor, I would call your mother and ask her to come and fetch you! But as I say, I've got a visitor. . . ." He continued in quite a different voice, looking nervously behind him, as if he expected the little vampire to appear. Hopefully he had long since made his escape!

He went on crossly, "Doctor's hours are over now! And besides, I have to go and attend to my visitor! Come back tomorrow morning."

Tony took his courage in both hands. "What about my pills?"

Dr. Rummage was obviously getting twitchy. "I'll fetch you a couple from my consulting room," he said. "Wait here."

Anxiously Tony watched him disappear into the room. For a moment he heard nothing. Then there was an uproar!

"The window!" Tony heard the doctor mutter, "I never thought of that. . . ."

Tony gave a little jump for joy. Now he knew for sure that the little vampire had made his escape. But he himself preferred not to meet Dr. Rummage at this very moment. . . .

He quickly turned and raced away. He ran down the garden path and pulled the gate shut behind him.

Only when he reached the bush where Anna had hidden the coffin did he stop.

But there was nothing there! No trace of Anna, or the little vampire! Only the flattened grass showed where the coffin had been.

Should he go on alone to the station in the hope of meeting Anna and Rudolph on the way? Forget it! The two vampires could manage just fine without him. He drew the scarf more tightly around his neck and ran back to the farm.

33 / If Your Mother's Still Around

Tony approached the farmhouse with an uneasy feeling. He strained his ears to listen, but no music came from the garden any longer: no murmur of voices, no laughter. Had the party already finished?

He noticed that a light was on in his room, and wondered if he had forgotten to switch it off. The front door was unlocked. As he crept quietly up the stairs, he could hear the television. Please let them all be sitting downstairs watching a movie! he prayed.

But as he cautiously opened the door of his room, the first thing he saw was his mother sitting on a chair by his bed.

"Hi, Mom!" he said as charmingly as he could.

She scowled but said nothing.

"Have you been here long?" He quickly slipped into his pajamas and got into bed.

"Where were you?" she asked sharply. Her voice sounded so angry that he winced.

"At the doctor's," he replied truthfully.

"I'm supposed to believe that, am I?"

"You can call him up."

"And what in the world were you doing there?"

"I wanted to get some different pills."

"You wanted . . ." she stopped. She obviously hadn't been prepared for that. "And I thought you were flitting about outside looking for vampires!"

"But, Mom!" he said. "I'm not *that* crazy!"

His mother studied him suspiciously. "Were you really with Dr. Rummage?"

"Yes!"

"Why didn't you tell us? We'd have gone to fetch the pills for you."

"I didn't want to bother you," he said craftily. His mother was particularly keen on politeness! "And fresh air is so healthy—that's what you keep telling me, anyway."

"Did you get the pills?"

"The pills? N-no. Dr. Rummage had—er—had another patient with him. But anyway, I don't need them anymore, I'm almost better."

"It's a pretty ridiculous story," said his mother, "but that's just why I believe it."

Tony made a reproachful face. "Why shouldn't it be true? Do you think I'd lie to you?" And it really wasn't a made-up story . . . Tony had just left out a few things that his mother mustn't find out about!

"Just when are we leaving tomorrow morning?" he asked to divert her attention. He sure hoped it would be before Dr. Rummage came by to see him!

"Straight after breakfast," answered his mother. "Dad's got to see a client in the afternoon."

Tony could have hugged her! But he couldn't let her see that, of course! "What a pity," he said in pretended disappointment.

"Have you enjoyed yourself here, then?" she asked in surprise.

"Yes," he lied.

"Didn't you miss all your vampires?"

"Wh-what do you mean?"

"Your funny friends who go around in vampire costumes?"

"Not at all," Tony assured her. How could I have missed them? he thought with a grin.

"In that case we can come back to the farm soon for another vacation!"

"That's fine with me," he said evenly. He couldn't have cared less what the future held in store at that moment.

"It's only your vampire books that you can't do without!" his mother remarked cuttingly.

"What do you mean?"

"You were in such a hurry to buy yourself that one in that store."

"So?"

"And you brought *Voices from the Vault* with you from home."

"If you say so."

"And I've found another idiotic vampire book you've hidden!"

Tony blanched. "Really? Which one?"

With a triumphant smile his mother produced from behind her back Anna's autograph book. "*Vampire Verses!*" she said, looking at the book with disgust.

"Have you looked inside it?" exclaimed Tony indignantly.

"Of course." She opened it. "Anna Emily Sackville-Bagg—is she a girl at your school? Her name seems familiar somehow."

"She—she's in fifth grade."

Tony's mother leafed through the book. "She's thought up some crazy names in here! William the Wild, Frederick the Frightful . . . are they supposed to be funny?" With a shake of her head she read, " 'Take care that on your lips/There's always fresh blood!' In my day we only wrote *nice* verses!"

"Times have changed," said Tony, who was delighted that she didn't seem to be taking the verses seriously.

She snapped the book shut and handed it to him. "And what are you going to write in it?"

Tony gave a broad grin.

"If your mother's still around
Be grateful through and through.
Lots of people in this world
Aren't as lucky as you!"

His mother was well aware of the sarcasm hidden in his voice as he said this verse. She stood up. "You really must be back to normal!" she said irritably, and left the room.

Tony gave a last glance at the autograph book, but he was too tired to think of another rhyme. He could do it tomorrow—on the way home.

34 / Sharing the Work

Tony came down to breakfast carrying the suitcase and backpack in which he had hidden the vampire books and the cape. He carried Anna's autograph book openly under his arm—there was no need to hide that anymore.

He found his mother in the dining room. She was sitting at the table with a cup of coffee in front of her, talking to the two ladies.

"Last night we slept really well for the very first time!" said one.

The other agreed with her. "It was blissfully quiet! What a shame you have to leave right now!"

"Yes, a real pity!" remarked Tony.

"Tony has completely changed his opinion of farms," explained his mother proudly. "Isn't that so, Tony? You've had fun after all."

"Certainly have," he said, without much risk, because out of the window he could see his father loading up the car.

"Luckily Tony will have music lessons to keep him busy," said his mother.

"Lucky me," said Tony. Then something occurred to him. "Do I absolutely have to take lessons this week?"

"Why ever shouldn't you?"

"Well, I am sick, after all."

"So you're sick, are you? Then we'd better wait and see Dr. Rummage."

"Er—I'm not *that* sick!" he assured her hastily. "In fact, I'm just fine really." That wasn't completely true, but he certainly didn't want to face Dr. Rummage again! "I can even take my suitcase out to the car by myself. And my backpack too."

With those words he gathered up his luggage and quickly left the room before his mother could remind him that he still hadn't eaten anything.

He put his things down next to the car.

"Are we leaving soon?" he asked.

"You just can't wait," grinned his father.

"Not at all," said Tony. He boldly added, knowing he had nothing to worry about, "If it were up to me, we'd stay here another week!"

His father seemed to take him seriously. "Unfortunately I've got to meet a client this afternoon," he explained. "So we really do have to leave—as soon as I'm ready."

The sooner the better! thought Tony.

"Can I help you?" he asked cheerfully.

"You can see where Mom is."

He bumped into his mother at the front door.

"Just look what Joanna's found!" she said, showing Tony the hat she was holding. "Isn't it just like yours? The same felt, the same green feather . . ."

Tony did his best not to give anything away. "Yes—it's very similar—" Of course, it *was* his hat, the one the little vampire had lost! "Where did she find it?" he asked.

"In with the horses, I think. Funny, it really could almost be your hat." With that she hung it by the coat hooks.

"Perhaps we should take it back with us," Tony suggested. "Just in case my hat ever gets lost."

His mother looked at him in surprise. "I thought you didn't like that hat."

"Oh, I do. Especially in winter." He could see for himself it wasn't a very convincing explanation.

"One hat's enough," his mother decided in any case. "Besides, it doesn't belong to us. Whoever owns it will come and fetch it sooner or later."

"Whatever you say," said Tony crossly. In that case it would be her fault when he could not produce it the next time he visited his grandmother, who had given it to him! Just to irritate her he asked: "Anyway—why are you leaving Dad to do all the work? You're the one who's always so keen on everybody pitching in!"

She threw him a poisonous look. "You would have to say something like that!"

He grinned. "I'm not the one who's always for sharing the work—you are!" he declared, and walked over to the car, head held high.

Mrs. Minnowpail and Joanna were waiting for him.

"I'm so glad you've enjoyed your stay," said Mrs. Minnowpail, without even asking him if he had. She looked at Joanna. "And we'd be very pleased if you would come and stay again—wouldn't we?"

Joanna nodded—and then turned red.

"Jeremy would be pleased too," went on Mrs. Minnowpail. "He's gone off shopping with my husband right now."

"If your children would ever like to visit us, we would be delighted to have them," Tony's mother said—also without having asked him!

"Oh, yes!" beamed Joanna.

"Oh, no!" groaned Tony.

"You mustn't pay too much attention to Tony," said his mother. "He's pretty shy. What's more, he hasn't had anything to eat today and that's why he's so grumpy." And she held out a Baggie. "Here. I've just made this for you. For the trip."

"Thanks," he growled, unwrapped a sandwich, and took a bite. That way at least he wouldn't be tempted to contradict her and keep the conversation going.

"Can't we go yet?" he asked ungraciously.

"You see?" laughed his mother. "He's always grouchy like this when his tummy's empty!"

35 / Vampires and Other Friends

"You made me out to be impossible!" Tony complained as soon as they were in the car.

"You think so?" said his mother, starting the engine.

Slowly they backed away past Mrs. Minnowpail and Joanna, who waved eagerly.

"Don't you agree you were grouchy?" asked his father.

"I had every reason to be!" Tony defended himself. "Why you had to invite them without even asking me . . . now I suppose they'll even have to sleep in my bedroom!"

"At least they're better than your vampire friends!" retorted his mother. "And I think it's time you found yourself some new friends."

"Well, I don't!" said Tony defiantly.

Secretly he had to admit she could be right. The little vampire really hadn't behaved the way a friend should! Tony only had to think of how they had carried the coffin to the train station together, and then the vampire never even said thank you at the end of it all! Or how Tony had practically saved his friend's life with the people who were waiting for their two visiting orphans, and the vampire had just squabbled with him, instead of being grateful and pleased! Or how, whenever it came to George the

Boisterous, the vampire simply twisted the facts to lay the blame on Tony!

You had to make allowances for the fact that being a vampire, he had a hard life and therefore had to think more of his own interests than a human would—but even so! Friendship meant that you didn't just think of yourself, but of the other person occasionally . . . like Anna did!

While he only felt cross and disappointed at Rudolph, the thought of Anna spread a warm glow over him. He opened the autograph book and read the verses through again. When he came to the page where *Tony* was written in Anna's childish handwriting, he suddenly knew what to write.

"Have you got something to write with?" he asked.

His father handed him a pen, and he wrote:

> *In cold Siberia lives the brown bear.*
> *Africa is the home of the gnu.*
> *Sicily shelters the wild boar so rare—*
> *But in my heart, there's room just for you!*
> From your *friend*, Tony

He underlined the word "friend" twice.

Contented and relieved, he leaned back in his seat. The little vampire would be bound to see the poem— and he would get downright annoyed! And he might even start acting a little more considerate, perhaps!

Tony's mother had been watching him in the rearview mirror. "That autograph book with its stupid rhymes just proves that they aren't good friends for you," she announced.

And his father asked, "When did you last go to volleyball practice, by the way?"

Tony hesitated. "About six months ago."

"Wouldn't you like to start going again? You used to enjoy it!"

"Hmmm. . . ."

"And what about your friend Ollie?" asked his mother. "Weren't you going to take a pottery course with him?"

"Yes, but—"

"Well, then! And you can give that autograph book right back to your friend in the vampire costume!"

Tony grinned to himself. If only it were as simple as that. . . . But the idea of the pottery course didn't seem so bad. You could always sculpt other things besides flower vases. Why not—vampires!

About the Author and Illustrator

ANGELA SOMMER-BODENBURG is the author of numerous short stories that have appeared in magazines and anthologies throughout the world, as well as several collections of poetry. Ms. Sommer-Bodenburg has written four books about Rudolph and Tony; *My Friend the Vampire, The Vampire Moves In, The Vampire Takes a Trip,* and *The Vampire on the Farm,* which are available in Minstrel Books.

AMELIE GLIENKE is a graphic artist and cartoonist. She is the illustrator of all the VAMPIRE stories.